THROUGH THE WRINGER

Edited by
Dean Wesley Smith

Stories from Pulphouse
FICTION MAGAZINE

WMG
PUBLISHING

Through the Wringer

Published by WMG Publishing Inc.
All stories reprinted from the pages of
Pulphouse Fiction Magazine
Cover and interior design copyright © 2024 WMG Publishing, Inc.
Cover art copyright © by studiostok | Depositphotos

ISBN 13 (Trade Paperback): 978-1-56146-998-7

MORE FROM PULPHOUSE

MORE STORIES FROM *PULPHOUSE FICTION MAGAZINE*

A Twist of a Knife

Alibi Murder

Aliens Among Us

Cattitude Edited

Destination Tomorrow or Yesterday

Don't Touch My Magic!

Ghosts Among Us

History Repeats for No Reason

Implode the Membrane

Jingle My Bells

No Way: Totally Twisted Tales

Run!! Creatures, Critters, and Pulphousers…

Snot-Nosed Aliens

That's Really Messed Up

There'll Be Blue Popcorn Without You!

Three Sheets to the Wind

Twisted Robots, Oh, My!

STORIES FROM THE ORIGINAL PULPHOUSE

Stories from the Original Pulphouse: A Fiction Magazine

Stories from Pulphouse: The Hardback Magazine

ALSO BY

DEAN WESLEY SMITH

COLD POKER GANG

Kill Game

Cold Call

Calling Dead

Bad Beat

Dead Hand

Freezeout

Ace High

Burn Card

Heads Up

Ring Game

Bottom Pair

Case Card

THE POKER BOY UNIVERSE

POKER BOY

The Slots of Saturn: A Poker Boy Novel

They're Back: A Poker Boy Short Novel

Luck Be Ladies: A Poker Boy Collection

Playing a Hunch: A Poker Boy Collection

A Poker Boy Christmas: A Poker Boy Collection

Dry Creek Crossing

Hot Springs Meadow

Green Valley

SEEDERS UNIVERSE

Dust and Kisses: A Seeders Universe Prequel Novel

Against Time

Sector Justice

Morning Song

The High Edge

Star Mist

Star Rain

Star Fall

Starburst

Rescue Two

CONTENTS

THROUGH THE WRINGER

INTRODUCTION

DEAN WESLEY SMITH

Back in the 2023 subscription drive for *Pulphouse Fiction Magazine*, we kept up a tradition of having stretch goals that were fun and off-the-beam anthologies of stories from issues of the magazine.

It seems that we hit five of the stretch goals last year, and as we went along putting it all together, I was coming up with titles that I thought would be fun to put Pulphouse stories under.

I never had a story or theme in mind with any of the titles, just the title and a fun cover. Or if I did have a theme, it is long now forgotten in the mists of the last year.

So I came at this title fresh and first thought I would use stories that put the characters through some sort of "wringer" or another. (You know, the devise used to take water out of wet clothes... yes, even before my time.)

But most great writers do that to their characters anyway. We professional writers tend to make it hard on our characters just to keep the story moving. So I took it to the next step. I decided that I would use stories that left the reader feeling wrung out in one fashion or another. Good or bad.

Actually I hope a few more good than bad.

And in typical Pulphouse fashion, the stories I picked crossed a bunch of genres.

I first thought of the fantastic Scott Edelman story "What Remains of America" from Issue #25. That brought me to the incredible Karen Fonville story "The Remarkable Way She Died" in the same issue, and then to Valerie Brook's amazing story "The Sea Girl's Survival" from the very first issue.

And from there the list of anthology stories just sort of fell into place.

I really had fun putting these stories together, revisiting some of these stunning works.

I sure hope you enjoy the read as well.

Dean Wesley Smith
Las Vegas, NV

LIVE THE PULPHOUSE LIFE!

Grab your Pulphouse mug and fill it with your favorite beverage and lounge in your coziest chair with the Thumper pillow while you read the latest issue of *Pulphouse*.

Want to mark off the date when your next issue will arrive? Get the *Pulphouse* calendar featuring some of our favorite *Pulphouse* cartoons!

Find all this and so much more at the *Pulphouse Fiction Magazine* online store at:

http://pulphousemagazine.com

THE PILLOW (22" X 22")

THE MUG (15 OZ.)

And say hi to Thumper while you're there.

THE SEA GIRL'S SURVIVAL

VALERIE BROOK

This is a new and original story from Valerie Brook, one of the best and most powerful new writers appearing on the scene. I have been lucky enough to purchase a few of her wonderful short stories.

Val's stories tend to get at the heart of the human condition in ways that very few writers can touch. Like a knife, she cuts to what drives and scares us.

"The Sea Girl's Survival" gives you a sense of the complexity and power of this wonderful writer. Enjoy.

THE SEA GIRL'S SURVIVAL

VAL BROOKS

The first time thirteen-year-old Abigale Oats heard the phantom whisper, the strange sloshing, wave-lapping *shhh* sound—she was biting her lip and trying not to cry at noon recess at Walter Luther Middle School.

Under the heat of New Mexico's desert-orange basketball sun, not a drop of liquid water anywhere for a mile except for the dirty, snake-winding Rio Grande; that *shhh* sound forced Abby to glance left and right.

Maybe the other kids had snuck up behind her again.

Like they had in the bathroom.

But only a sea of crispy brown grass surrounded Abby, and the lonely pockmarked baseball field like a crater on a desolate moon, and an Earless lizard that did pushups in the powdery dirt whenever Abby looked at it.

You, too, can exercise.

Walter Luther didn't even *have* a stupid baseball team.

Only the beheaded, skeletal tumbleweeds ran the

3

diamond, with their berserkers gait and regardless of rules at all.

The air smelled of the yellow chamiso field beyond the broken chain-link fence; the wild bush that locals said was stinky as feet and caused seasonal allergies, and the tourists thought was the epitome of an exotic desert fragrance.

The air right now was definitely nasty like a bloated fish rotting in an athlete's shoe. Abby might be brand new to the Southwest, but she had a local person's nose.

The dead fingers of the breathless September breeze, which was too hot and tired to push anything of substance, brushed only the finest hairs on Abby's neck under her short, curly mop of sweaty hair.

If hair can sweat.

The other seventh-graders played on the concrete school-yard—where the basketball hoops stood tall, just like rust-colored dinosaur bones with netted, slack-hung jaws—the kids all laughing and shouting, their voices pushing the distance toward Abby through a shimmery sky curtain of heat waves.

But no one looked at her on the forbidden metallic bleachers. No one waved. No one said: Hey friend, what are you doing sitting out there all alone; are you okay?

Abby hunched on the fry-pan hot aluminum—which hadn't seemed too hot until she plunked down on the metal, and then after the burn of surprise, the pain felt alright.

As if her physical pain and emotional pain were natural born enemies, and would have a boxing fistfight inside her body, and the physical pain would win in a knockout.

Be the champion of her torment.

And then her stupid emotional tears would suck back in

defeat, and she'd have on her normal face again; the one that could talk and smile without her big lip quivering.

Mr. Rodrigues in fifth-period math always called on her; because the Hispanics chewed gum, and the Indians passed paper notes. And that one Asian boy stuttered.

But Abby just learned math.

The bottom side of her fleshy thighs were probably getting a horizontal bacon imprint, or turning into pinched-up skin corduroy, because she'd been stupid enough to wear shorts. Not that shorts were stupid, but it was because she'd forgotten to shave her legs.

Looking ever so hairy and unpopular; and like an Anglo person from Alaska, too.

Because Anglo was unpopular. (And Alaska was total outer space.)

Actually, she basically had two skin colors: College-paper white or boiled-lobster red. Plus freckles and shocked out ginger hair. Which she could have done well, if she'd been reinvented as a fat clown, and liked spoiled children. And was a creepy man.

Abby pinched her eyes closed.

There was no way the *shhh* sound could be real. No cell phone speakers to trick her. Nobody whispering behind her.

And it wasn't her own heartbeat. Couldn't be. It just didn't have the rhythm of a heart.

It sounded like a real, wet, blue sea.

———

The second time Abby heard the watery *shhh* sound, it was dark in the guest bedroom where she was wrapped up deep in itchy wool blankets on the rickety metal bed.

So dark black, that the darkness became a moody creature that exhaled its smoky pinon breath over her face when the red glow flickered out down the hall in the kiva fireplace—where step-grandfather Mesta cooked posole and beans—and then she couldn't tell if her eyes were really open or closed tight.

She might be swallowed by dark, be inside the digestive stomach juices of dark.

Churning around and around.

But when her eyes got dry; that's when she knew they were open to the air.

And staring at nothing but blackened memory; the squat room that had only an empty wooden dresser, the mug of Bic pens, the beeswax candle, and her messy traveler's suitcase stuffed inside the small, barren closet which was filled with everything she could carry.

The class-action lawyers and the social workers had the rest of her family's stuff in storage somewhere back in Alaska. Because the case had gone bigwig; had gone hush-tones and important.

And Mesta kept the legal correspondences hidden, maybe in a clever, manila folder. Slid in a furniture crevasse somewhere. Abby had tried to look around his house—but just with her eyes, not with her fingers.

She was a teleported stranger here.

At the dinner table awkward Mesta always mumbled, let's not talk of it now.

If not now, then *when?*

Mesta's adobe stank of cinnamon mouthwash. The smell had built up in Abby's nose—and even when she closed the bathroom door across from her bedroom, the mouthwash still ghosted through the air to haunt her.

Mesta had a gingivitis bone infection thing.

He was like super old. And when he spit in the sink, it wasn't always the sink.

A kindly man for sure, his eyes were soft and brown, especially when he said he didn't know where Abby's grandmother had gone, except she'd gone tropical when he stayed desert.

Left him on an adventure a year ago, but they didn't divorce, because they loved each other and she still sent him monthly checks.

So those lawyers were on it, making business-suit lawyerly calls. Until they located biological Grandma, Abby was stuck with non-biological Mesta—which got really confusing overall because he didn't even—because all the rest of Abby's biological family was—

—No.

Because of stupid deluxe new minivans that can seat the whole family except her, because she had the flu, for the hockey game; and mountain cliffs, and faulty class-action brakes.

And four funerals.

Practically overnight, Abby was put on a crowded commercial flight, stuffed into a seat like a cow, and sent to temporarily stay here in the stupid cinnamon-mouthwash barn where Mesta booted her out in the morning to graze, and the school booted her home in the afternoon back to her stall.

Where she stared at the plastered walls in her room. And followed the cracks with her eyes.

And Mesta hardly spoke much English though he spoke it just fine.

She couldn't even have a TV out here. No cell phone. And she hated to read.

And the blue watery *shhh* sound came back in the pitch dark.

Whispered up through the lumpy chicken feather pillow, through the cotton mattress, the mud brick floor. Up through the solid dark earth a thousand miles beneath her, until all that hard earth sloshed into real salty water.

Rocked her gently in her bed, and she opened her eyes, and the sun flared in a coppery-white flash. Her lips tasted of brine.

And on her cheeks, she felt a sticky, sea-salt hairspray.

The dream was of a turquoise ocean, and a big orange floating raft. And how Abby lay there on the boat bottom, her legs rolling back and forth, in and out of consciousness; her face slowly turning lobster red.

W hy go to school.

Why not wander *away* from the 7:15 am bus stop, where Abby stood alone at the crossroads between this dirt road and that other dirt road, with a heavy backpack of school books, most of which she had only opened accidentally.

She crunched on the side of the road for twenty minutes in her brown leather piano loafers, which were too small and her feet bulged out, and cars passed now and then and made her cough in dust.

She rolled her ankle once and had to sit down and rub it.

The dust stuck to her shaved and moisturized legs.

Irritated red bumps flushed her calves.

All around New Mexico it was brown. And flat, or hilly and shrubby, and rocky where poisonous rattlesnakes could lay.

And there weren't even any famous green cactus she could see.

It was like God had made every other world ecosystem with care, and then it was the end of the sixth day and he was running late, so he just threw the creation leftovers out here like recycling.

The blue-sky forehead of the morning frowned with concern and watched Abby through its cyclopean sun eye, as if it might call in some mythic herding dogs to nip her ankles, to get her back into the bus line.

But a line of one unpopular person is not much of a line.

The river Rio Grande: It was sandy ground, woody debris, muddy olive water that flowed soft like someone had left on their backyard hose and then magnified the effect into a whole long river that cut the Southwest in half.

A canopy of Cottonwood trees, thick brown trunks and orange fiery leaves cast a bedazzled shade; and Abby plunked down on the embankment to listen to the wide water gurgle and flow.

She unzipped her backpack, and the zipper bit her thumb.

Pulled out a purple cube of sugary gum to smack. Oh, but first a mint chocolate square. The mint made her ears tingle, and a languid breeze fingered her hair.

She dropped her school books into the water, let them float away. One by one, they were like a row of ducklings without a mother.

Even the math book swept away. Bye-bye math.

When Abby crunched back along the dirt road to Mesta's adobe, her backpack was light as air. Her shoulders were boingy springs.

"How was school," Mesta mumbled at the bean and posole dinner.

"Okay."

———

T hat night in the bed, in the dark, was the third time Abby heard the watery *shhh* sound, and it came on so loud, and so fast—it sucked her all the way out of New Mexico in a flash.

She opened her eyes to the coppery flare of sunlight blinding her eyes.

Her vision streaked into a whiteout: But she remembered the slippery bottom of the orange boat, and her legs rocking back and forth, and how the salty sea spray itched inside her nose.

Riding the bed of an endless ocean.

"*Shhh,*" a French woman spoke into Abby's ear. "It's okay, honey. It's okay."

"What's okay?" Abby asked.

The cyclopean sun's eye had her transfixed in a blinding ray. And a sweet metal tinge of blood coated her lips. "Why do you keep saying that?"

"*Jamais deux, sans trois.* Never twice, without thrice. It's okay, we will prepare." The small, minty hands of the unseen woman massaged Abby's burned face with paste, and fresh water slid down her throat. And when she woke up, Abby was back in bed in New Mexico in the early dawn.

With dried blood from where she had chewed her lip.

She didn't go to school.

Big puffy clouds roamed the wide desert sky as Abby cut through the pinon trees and trudged in her piano loafers to the bank of the Rio Grande.

For a second she swore she saw a rattlesnake, but it was just a stick. Her heart pounded. She had to find a grassy place to sit down all alone.

And that's when the emotional boxer stood up in the boxing ring like the Comeback King; and waves of grief pummeled Abby in the gut and she sobbed and sobbed, snot hanging out her nose in two thin ropes.

"I can't do it alone," she cried. Over and over, until she curled up on her side. Sand stuck to the snot on her cheek, and she thought: It's not sandpaper, it's *skin*paper. And it was gross.

When she sat up again, Abby was lighter. Her chest felt like it did when she got off the Ferris wheel at the fair.

That was a good memory. The Alaska State fair every year. Wow, the deep-fried meat coma, the classic aging rockers on stage, the lumberjack show and the Peninsula Racing Pigs. Even the RV and boat storage display. Ha-ha, and the twins won the cabbage weigh-off.

So funny.

Abby nudged off her loafers and dipped her toes into the Rio Grande. It was lukewarm, like a forgotten bath.

It was nice and refreshing, though. She waded into a soft

and shallow bottom, and the mud swirled up and buried her feet. She sat down. And the river saturated her shorts and her underwear and she felt so daring, like a rule breaker.

A daredevil.

The mud swallowed her legs.

When she walked home, her piano loafers squeaking, her pants rolled up to the knees; the social worker, the one with a moustache, sat with a clipboard on the dash of his forest green Subaru, with a cell phone pushed against his ear, and his eyes not quite the color of Alaskan ice.

———

In school again; at noon recess, on the same hot bleachers.

When the *shhh* came, Abby squinted up at the cyclopean eye in the sky and said, "Just take me."

"God won't take us, honey," the woman on the raft said.

"Why?"

The big orange boat bobbed up and down and the endless turquoise ocean had turned choppy gray. Clouds swirled overhead like a giant might slowly be wielding a metal whisk, preparing to pour in more sky ingredients, maybe some thunder to rumble.

Abby managed to pull herself up on her elbows, the firm raft's edge supporting her neck. The air smelled like electricity.

The French woman in a bedraggled business suit sat beside Abby, arms and legs loose like a ragdoll, one sleeve torn off like a punk-rocker, and a white bra strap overstretched and sagging on her shoulder. Her wet, flat hair looked ironed to her face. One eye was swollen shut like a dark walnut.

"Jamais deux, sans trois." The French woman studied the angering sky, a warm wind fingering her battered clothing, fluttering the edges of the fabric. "You are my good luck charm, Abigale Oats."

Abby felt bothered.

Something familiar was missing. She was wrapped in plastic, and couldn't feel. That's it—numb and thick as rubber. Abby's body all over was numb.

"Why am I dreaming of dying on a raft?"

"You're not dreaming, honey." The French woman's voice floated away.

"Then how come I don't stay here?"

The French woman pulled her face away from the sky, as if she had been magnetically transfixed. The gathering storm reflected and swirled in her wild eyes. "No one stays here." And she reached out with her little hands, and grabbed Abby's hand, and it felt like she would never let go.

The fabric above her sleeveless arm went *pat-a-pat-a-pat.*

Abby yanked the covers off her bed. The creature that was the darkness shrank back as Abby struck a match and lit the beeswax candle on the dresser. The flame danced in shadows on the wall.

"Where is real?" she whispered to the dark. "You? Are you real?"

The candle flared, and the darkness turned and ran with its tail between its legs. Abby's bare toes gripped the smooth brick tiles of the floor. Mesta's old man snore carried down the hall. She yanked a wool blanket off the bed and wrapped it around her shoulders Indian style.

Carried the candle in its ceramic holder in one hand, squeezed the blanket closed in the other hand, and shuffled quietly to the front door; then out onto the still sun-warm flagstone porch, the blue-black night with the stars sneezed out overhead, and glistening with fuzzy, twinkling light.

The air smelled of creosote and sage.

Abby set the candle down on the sundial planter box.

Was she dead, too? This could be, like—the process of the afterworld where you work things through?

And the thought of the hidden manila envelope with the lawyers' correspondence came to mind, and that it was time to use her fingers to find it. So she slunk around the adobe house with her candle, trying not to light herself on fire, or wake up the sleeping snorer. And *nowhere* was the manila that she could find.

It was only an afterthought: The mailbox.

So back out into the blue-black, star-sneezed night, in her piano loafers and crunching over the gravel driveway to the rusty metal mailbox propped up on a stick.

It squeaked open.

There lay a crisp white letter.

Ten minutes later, cross-legged on her bed with the candle flickering on the dresser: Abby knew her grandmother had been found by the high-tech lawyers. And she held the one-way ticket to Honolulu in her shaking hands. Business first class.

The flight left in one day.

Abby's heart pounded in her ears.

Jamais deux, sans trois. So the plane would crash over the water. Impossible! The second tragedy in her life, and bad things came in threes. But not if she could warn them—warn everyone.

When dawn broke the night, and the snoring stopped and the toilet flushed, and Mesta had his steaming cuppa joe at the kitchen table—Abby slunk out of the guest room and pulled out a wooden chair to sit across from him.

The chair's legs were uneven. It tilted back and forth with a soft *clonk* on the tiles until she sat rigidly upright.

Sausage sizzled crazily in a pan.

"I'm suposta go to Hawaii tomorrow but we have to reschedule it." Abby pushed the letter across the table, but she kept the ticket inside the envelope, clasp in her hand.

Mesta took a century to read the letter with his reading glasses perched low on his nose. He got up and flipped the pigs in the pan, then shuffled to Abby and handed her the letter back personally, then sat down in his spot.

"Why don't you have a phone," she said.

He took a long coffee sip, and looked at Abby with kindly brown eyes. "I'm peculiar." That was his explanation.

Abby leaned forward and the broken chair gave a loud *clonk*. She put her hand over her mouth so she wouldn't shout, because she suddenly felt like shouting.

"They want you in the school," he said. "But why listen to them? Your last day in the *desierto*, and a fine one it should be."

Abby thought that maybe a hundred random people were going to die tomorrow. Crashed at sea. And a fine day this last one would not be.

She rushed to school.

She asked to see the principal, but he was out today. She

found Mr. Rodriguez in the hallway, and showed him the letter, and tried to say that the plane might crash, but Mr. Rodriquez just said, I will miss you in class, you bright young lady.

She talked the front desk secretary into handing her the push button phone. But when the airplane operator came on, and said how may I help you—Abby hung up instead.

At recess she sat on the hot aluminum bleachers only long enough to scan the playground, to make sure no one was looking, and then she escaped through the broken chain-link fence into the yellow chamiso field.

She didn't even think of the stinky feet smell. She just clutched the envelope to her chest.

The bushes tickled her sensitive legs.

The front seam on her left piano loafer broke open, and her toe squeezed out and pinched on a rock.

"Maybe it's not a second chance," she whispered. She looked up into the cyclopean portal in the sky; into the white-out, into the doorway in her mind.

———

Rain howled and roared in a slate gray tempest, ocean spray kicked Abby's face with needles. The French woman got dunked, her wet hair became an iron helmet over her face; in the metallic flash of lightening, a medieval knight-in-armor.

Screaming inside a faceless shell.

Up and down the raft bucked.

Abby's legs swishing far left, then far right.

And she couldn't hold onto the life rope.

Anymore.

A bby lay down in the chamiso field, on her back, under a canopy of thirsty flowers. The hard dirt. The feeling of being invisible, and not having to do anything.

If I die there, will I vanish here?

But she thought long and hard about it again—about being in two real places, and the doorway opening and closing. And she decided that one place had to be unreal.

Had to be a sideways place. Another land. A mental landscape.

But which one, the future or the past?

Oh Jesus, but what if a rattlesnake comes by. Abby rolled up on her elbows and then rolled over to her knees and then stood up all covered with dust.

Suddenly, the field was creepy, with too many rocky places for poisonous things to hide. She didn't want to be in the creepy field.

She didn't want to be in New Mexico, even.

She wanted to be in Alaska, before the—

Before everything went to shit.

And it seemed suddenly that Abby had never directly asked for what she needed. Had never thought she could. Had never dared dream it possible. But *now* she dared.

Because it was almost too late.

She was letting go of the rope in the real world.

"Mommy, come help me," she cried. "Come here and help me. I need you. I can't live without you."

A figure materialized, standing in the golden field, the sun a perfect halo around her familiar shape, the golden light pouring out from behind her.

And Abby ran to her mother's outstretched arms, and she cried until the sorrow turned to wonderment, and then to joy —and then into the wisdom of *knowing*.

The sky rotated to night, because they needed to walk among the mysteries of the stars: Because the stars hold the secrets of all things.

And all souls journey.

Destiny awaits you sweet child, and though I can no longer be with you physically on Earth—my love, I will never leave your side.

There are souls who await your return. There are promises you have made, lives you must intersect, people only you can help save.

Will you abandon them now? The choice is yours. For as you choose it; it will be.

And what will not be remembered, will never be lost.

———————

The tempest sea had turned into a lonely, calm, blue bath.

The life raft had mostly deflated.

One compartment of air inside the orange rubber still gallantly buoyed. Abby and the French woman clung to it, the white safety rope. Had their hands and arms wrapped around it.

And all together they were a giant's wrung-out bath toy— abandoned, left to sink down into an oceanic drain.

"I'm a curse," Abby said.

"No, no—not that way," the French woman laughed. "You *survived* three times. You *survived*."

And the positive side of the meaning sank in, and Abby laughed, because she felt like a wine cork, bobbing up and down as they drifted. "You're my new lawyer from across the isle on the plane. And you apologized about the firm, and me being sent to Mesta. And you were explaining my case."

"Hi, I'm Claudine."

"I'm Abigale."

And they both laughed so much with the wild absurdity that they almost drown, but they held each other up above the bath of warm, turquoise water; and laughed more and more.

After awhile they were quiet again.

Claudine glanced at her watch, which had stopped telling time. "We missed the meeting at Santon and Fischer."

"That line out there, see the shimmer rising up. See the brown?" Abby asked.

"I think that's the big island we're floating to. We were not that far out when the sea crash happened."

Wow, it was an island sanctuary in the middle of all the nothingness. And Abby felt like she needed to remember something important, but floating with her chin barely above the sea, nothing else came to mind.

Except the overpowering will to live.

No matter what.

Then they heard Coast Guard rescue helicopter blades chopping the sky.

SEEING HIM FOR THE FIRST TIME

DAVID H. HENDRICKSON

David H. Hendrickson sometimes leaves his award-winning mystery worlds and ventures over into a form of social commentary. And he does it here with this fantastic original story that very much fits this time and place.

His short fiction has appeared in Best American Mystery Stories 2018, Ellery Queen's Mystery Magazine, Heart's Kiss, *and numerous anthologies, including over a half dozen issues of* Fiction River.

SEEING HIM FOR THE FIRST TIME

DAVID H. HENDRICKSON

Janice McManus had seen him before, of course. They were both juniors at Lynn English High School, a school of fifteen hundred students located in a tough, blue-color city north of Boston. Janice even shared a Social Studies class with him. But until that moment, she hadn't really *seen* him. He'd been no more than a part of the background of her life.

There, but not really *there*. Inconsequential. One of *them*, not one of *us*.

And then, on a day that had been like any other, she truly saw Nate Crawford for the first time. She was walking alone down the long, dusty, corridor from Math class to Social Studies, pushing past the fire doors, her two books pinned against her chest, wearing her favorite light yellow dress with small white butterflies. It was her shortest dress, two inches above the knee, but considering the style here in 1967 and what many of the other girls wore, it still could be considered reasonably modest. Certainly not the type of micro-mini that insured girls front-row seats in Dirty Old Man Ferguson's class. She was pretty in a quiet sort of way, petite, with long brown hair.

The corridor, painted an industrial green with gray lockers running along both sides, was crowded with students walking two- and three-abreast in both directions. The buzz of conversation and an occasion burst of laughter filled the air along with stray scents of perfume, cologne, and stale sweat.

A day like any other. Until Janice felt a hand sweep across her butt, and give it a good squeeze.

Janice whirled. Outraged, she glared at Phil Drake, star of the basketball team, a lanky 6-3, with a mop of jet black hair. He stared back in mock innocence, but a smile tugged at both corners of his mouth.

"What do you think you're doing?" Janice demanded.

"What are you talking about?" he said, spreading his bare hands wide. But he couldn't hold back the leering smile.

Just like he'd done the last time. And the time before that. Each time denying with his words what he acknowledged with his leer.

"I'm going to report you," Janice said, as other students veered around them into the middle of the corridor, some slowing to watch.

"Report what?" Drake said. "That I grabbed your ass? Like you claimed a month ago, and the month before that, too? Hey, it's a crowded corridor. People accidentally bump into each other and touch each other all the time. Face it, you're a psycho. Fixated on me." He stabbed himself in the chest with one finger for emphasis. "Hell, I can do better than you without trying. You probably *wish* I'd grab your ass."

Janice felt her throat tighten, and her mouth grow dry. She

tried to swallow, but couldn't. She glanced at the stares of passing students and felt her face grow hot.

With a smirk, Drake turned to leave, but first nodded at her chest and fired off one last shot. "Are those tits or mosquito bites?"

He laughed, and shouldered past her, unbelievably *brushing his hand across her butt one more time.*

Janice gasped.

Then stared in wonder as Nate Crawford—black, slender, and no more than 5-10 with a few of those inches his huge Afro—rushed past. He stepped in front of Drake, blocking his way.

The two collided, then squared off to face each other, sideways to Janice.

"What the hell do you think you're doing?" Drake demanded.

"I saw what you did," Nate said, his voice still carrying a distinct Southern drawl even though his family had moved to Massachusetts from Mississippi what had to be two or three years ago. "Man, that ain't cool."

"Listen to you, Deputy Dawg!" Drake said, using the exaggerated drawl of the Southern, Saturday morning cartoon character. "Why don't you just run along and chase some varmints."

"That wasn't right, what you did," Nate said. "You think you can just do stuff like that and get away with it?"

"I always do," Drake said with a smug smile. He crossed his arms and raised an eyebrow. "Now what are you gonna do about it? You're just a little black boy who couldn't even make the basketball team. Imagine that. One of your kind who can't play ball worth a lick. You're a disgrace to your own race. You know that, *boy*?"

Nate took a deep breath and slowly licked his lips. "We'll see what the principal has to say."

A flicker of fear flashed through Drake's eyes then was gone, replaced by the usual smug defiance.

"You're going to report *me* to the principal?" Drake again stabbed himself in the chest with a finger for emphasis. "For doing what? Bumping into her? You can't be serious." And with a dismissive wave, and the worst of racial epithets muttered under his breath, he was off.

Nate turned to Janice. The students who had slowed or stopped to watch the confrontation moved along, most with disappointed looks.

"Are you okay?" Nate asked. The sweetness and concern in his brown eyes took Janice's breath away.

Not that anything even faintly romantic could possibly happen between them. She was white; he was black. Yes, this was Massachusetts, not Mississippi. True, it was the middle of March, 1967, not back in the Dark Ages before the start of the Civil Rights movement. And she believed in equality, no matter what awful things her father said about black people. She could even see herself marching with Dr. Martin Luther King someday.

But the thought of a black boyfriend had never even occurred to her. Equal rights was one thing, *that* was another.

Until now. Not because she'd been the maiden in distress and Nate had come to her rescue like a knight in shining armor. Just that his actions had opened her very closed eyes.

Now, for the first time, she really saw him. He was good looking. Unblemished, chocolate-colored skin. A nice smile.

And that huge Afro did look good on him even if it did set off people like her father. Most of all, though, Nate seemed like a nice person. A gentleman, to use that old-fashioned word her parents so often trotted out. She hadn't noticed that in the few years she'd gone to school with Nate because her eyes had been closed. He'd been one of *them*.

But he seemed like a genuinely nice person, a gentleman. And based on her recent run of boyfriends, one good-looking jerk after another, she found a *gentleman* to be awfully attractive.

Especially one who also looked good, and had the kindest brown eyes she'd ever seen.

But what was she thinking?

It was impossible.

Nate took his seat at the right rear of the Social Studies classroom, disappointed that Janice, who sat diagonally ahead of him in the second row on the left, had decided not to go to the principal.

"Thank you for helping me, but I don't want to make a big scene," she'd said back in the hallway, looking away.

"You don't have to make a big scene. Just tell the principal what happened, and I'll say I saw it, too. It's the only way to get him to stop."

"Yes, but..." She shook her head, but said nothing more.

"What?"

"They won't believe me. They'll just say it was accidental, like he says. Phil Drake is their golden boy. They're going to believe him over me."

"Even if I saw it, too?"

"If they believe us, they'll... they'll say it's my fault because my dress is too short."

Nate glanced over, even though he knew exactly how short her yellow dress with white butterflies was. He made sure not to look too long. "It's a beautiful dress."

Janice flushed. "Thank you. But it's also my shortest one and—"

"Plenty of girls wear them shorter," Nate said, then wished he'd kept his big mouth shut. He wasn't sure how much he should admit to have noticed the shortness of the miniskirts on either Janice or other girls.

"But they'll still say it's my fault," Janice said. "Maybe even talk to my parents."

And that had ended the discussion. Janice thanked him again, and they took their seats. Silver-haired Miss Litchfield called the class to order, and the twenty-eight students—white except for three other blacks and two Spanish—fell silent.

Even more than usual, Nate couldn't get Janice out of his mind. He had thought she was beautiful and sweet and intelligent for as long as he could remember. In another world, he'd have thought he was in love with her.

But a large part of him had never left Mississippi. Born and raised in Yazoo City, he'd lived there until three years ago. And in Yazoo City, you knew better than to even *look* at a white girl. About the time his family up and left Mississippi, the bodies of James Chaney, Andrew Goodman, and Michael Schwerner were just being found in the swamps where the KKK lynch mob had left them, along with so many others.

Trying to register black people to vote in Mississippi had been their death sentence. Down there, black and white people didn't eat in the same restaurants, sleep in the same hotels, use the same rest rooms, or drink from the same water fountains. Young black men were told at an early age, and in no uncertain terms, that they were not to even *think* about white girls.

The specter of the KKK still haunted Nate, though he'd presumably left it far behind. Here in Lynn, less than an hour north of Boston, no one got lynched, and everyone used the same rest rooms and restaurants, and the schools were at least theoretically integrated, based on neighborhoods, with Lynn English mostly white and Lynn Classical far more dominated by blacks.

But if any black young men dated white girls even here in Massachusetts, that was news to him. Maybe there were some famous black athletes who were exceptions that proved the rule, but if they were out there, they weren't publicizing the fact.

So Nate knew that he should really stop thinking of Janice. He had no chance at winning her heart. None at all.

And what if by some miraculous fluke she ever did fall for him even remotely as hard as he'd fallen for her? It could go nowhere. They had less of a chance than Romeo and Juliet. The Montagues and Capulets had nothing over whites and blacks in this country.

What's more, until today, she'd acted as though he didn't even exist. Or at least barely existed. Just another faceless member of the student body.

Until today.

She'd certainly noticed him today. And had even... had that actually been some sliver of affection in her eyes?

No, it couldn't be. Not after three years of ignoring him. It had just been gratitude for him standing up for her. A switch hadn't suddenly been flicked on, letting her know that he was out there.

Loving her.

No, no, no, no, no. What was he thinking? How could he even use the L word in the same sentence with her? Even if it was true, he needed to put all thoughts of her aside.

All thoughts of *Janice, Janice, Janice.*

He realized he was looking at her now, up there on the far left in the second row. He'd probably been staring at her since the start of class, staring like some kind of creep. He certainly hadn't heard a word Miss Litchfield had been saying.

Trying not to think of Janice was impossible, but he'd just have to do it. Find some other girl to think about. A black girl, of course. There were plenty of them that were pretty, smart, and amusing. Cicely Jones. Kelly Thompson. Danielle Mitchell. All nice girls. He'd gone out on dates with all of them, and had a good enough time. Plenty of laughs.

They just weren't Janice.

He'd wind up taking one of them to the junior prom next month. Probably Cicely. His Momma would approve, and so would his three younger sisters.

Cicely. He'd ask her to the movies this weekend. And if they had a good time, maybe ask her to the prom then. Yes, that would be the big step he needed to take to get Janice out of his mind. He was happy to have stood up for her against Phil Drake. A girl shouldn't have to put up with that kind of groping. But that was as far as things would go with her.

He'd done the right thing. Now it was time—long *past* time —to do the sensible thing, and forget Janice.

If he could.

B efore school started the next morning, Janice made her way to Nate Crawford's locker, her heart in her throat. She couldn't believe what she was about to do. She was wearing a navy blue skirt and a peach-colored ruffled blouse, and held two textbooks to her chest. Nate turned and smiled shyly. He was wearing black slacks, matching shoes, and a dark blue, button-down shirt.

Janice looked down at her shoes, and wondered if she should just run away. It would be the safe thing to do, the thing any girl in her position with silly ideas should do.

She swallowed hard and tried to begin. "I want to thank you again for what you did yesterday."

Nate smiled that beautiful, warm smile. "You've thanked me more than enough. I was just doing what was right."

"Well, yeah. I guess." Janice smiled awkwardly. "I was wondering..." A lump formed in her throat. "I thought..." She took a deep breath, trying to calm the pounding in her chest. Was this was a heart attack was like? She felt a bead of sweat form on her forehead. Afraid she was about to chicken out, she forced the words from her mouth. "I was thinking maybe you'd like to get something to eat after school."

Nate's jaw dropped. His eyes widened.

I knew this was a bad idea! What a disaster! Panic flooded over her. She turned to run away in humiliation, when she saw Nate nod, ever so slightly at first, then rapidly and with enthusiasm.

Really? He was saying yes? Really?

Janice tried to control her racing thoughts, darting about in every direction. She licked her lips.

"I've got my Mom's car, so we could go for a roast beef at Bill & Bob's, or a pizza at Fauci's. Or just some fries or an ice cream at Friendly's. Even a donut at Mrs. Foster's if that's what you'd like."

"Sure," Nate said with a strangled sound that made Janice suddenly wonder if he was as nervous as she was, as impossible as that was to imagine.

"My treat," Janice said, then, when Nate began to shake his head, wondered if that had been the wrong thing to say at all.

"I can pay," he said, then patted his pants pocket as if making sure he had enough.

The words that this was her way of saying thank you almost escaped her lips. But she avoided that blunder—hadn't he said she'd already thanked him enough, and wasn't this invitation more than just a thank you?—only to say something even worse.

"It's not like a date or anything," she said, and wanted to cry out in agony because wasn't that exactly what she'd wanted, or at least maybe so, only under the camouflage of a thank you?

And when something—disappointment?—flashed in Nate's eyes at those words, Janice almost screamed out her frustration.

"No, of course not," Nate said, but his weak smile and the shaking in his voice belied the words.

"I'll meet you in the parking lot out back after school," Janice said, and rushed away before she ruined anything else.

———

I t was the longest school day in Nate's life. Each time he looked up at a classroom clock, it seemed to have moved only fifteen seconds. He didn't see Janice in the hallways, and didn't have Social Studies that day, and soon he began to wonder if it had all been a hallucination.

Or the most cruel of practical jokes.

He couldn't imagine Janice doing that to him. Other girls, maybe, but not her. He even knew of a white girl in Mississippi that had set up almost the exact same thing only for it to be a trap and the boy had been beaten to within an inch of his life.

But this wasn't Mississippi, he told himself. And Janice wasn't at all like that other girl. Although he had to admit, until yesterday, Janice had given him no reason to believe in her.

Well, none of that mattered. He loved Janice—there was that *love* word again!—and if he couldn't trust her, then life wasn't much worth living.

With his heart aflutter, he made his way to the rear exit, put on his dark blue windbreaker, and stepped out onto the parking lot. A brisk wind blew in his face. Nate looked all about.

Saw no sign of Janice.

His heart sank. It had been sick practical joke after all.

Suddenly, a horn beeped, and an old gray Rambler pulled up beside him. It was a box-like car with no stylish angles whatsoever. A grandma car, seemingly designed to be as ugly as possible. The anti-Corvette.

But Janice was inside, sitting behind the steering wheel, leaning over to open the passenger side door for him.

"Hop in, handsome!" she called cheerfully.

Nate ducked inside and slid onto the bench-like seat.

"It's a Mom-mobile, but it works," Janice said, and they both laughed.

They decided on pizza at Fauci's, and five minutes later, they walked inside and ordered. The air smelled pleasantly of tomato and garlic, and of flour and freshly tossed dough. The cashier, a middle-aged, gum-chewing woman with her hair up in a bun, rang up the sale on the cash register, and Janice and Nate split the bill. There were two rows of six booths and tables. They chose the row set back from the front glass window that overlooked Wyoma Square, and took the booth furthest from the door, Nate sliding into the side facing the door.

"I want to apologize," Janice said, clasping her hands on the red-and-white checked table. "For the past several years, since you moved here, I haven't been as... as friendly as I should have been. I wasn't unfriendly, but I never really—"

"—knew I existed," Nate blurted out.

His hand shot to his mouth in horror, and Janice's eyes widened, as he was sure his had as well.

"I am so sorry," he said, instinctively reaching out to touch her hand to reassure her that he hadn't meant to say that.

Janice's eyes widened even more.

Nate yanked his hand away from hers as if it had been a blistering hot stove, even though the skin on the back of her hand had been smooth and cool, and quite pleasant to the touch.

"I am so, so sorry," he said, his heart practically exploding out of his chest. "I swear I didn't mean to—"

"No, that was nice," Janice said.

"What?"

"Could you put your hand back on mine?" she said softly, her cheeks flushing with a tinge of crimson. "That was nice. Unless, of course, you don't want to."

Nate had all he could do to keep from grabbing her hand with a ferocity that would scare her away for sure. Instead, he placed the palm of his hand over the back of hers. He felt its softness for an instant, then she turned her hand, and their palms clasped.

The way that lovers held each other's hands.

"I never considered this, you holding my hand," Janice said softly. "You were on the other side of a mental fence. It took your actions yesterday for me to see that the fence even existed, and to know how worthless it is. I'm sorry that was what it took to open my eyes." She squeezed his hand. "Does any of that make sense?"

Nate had barely followed her words, his mind and heart instead locked onto the feel of her hand clasped to his, the smoothness of her skin, and the softness of her voice. But he'd followed the words enough. "Sure," he said, nodding.

"If I'm being too forward—"

"No," he said, shaking his head now. "No, not at all."

"Here's your pizza!" announced the gum-chewing cashier, appearing out of nowhere with the steaming hot pizza on a silver circular tray, supported by an orange rectangular tray that also held two glasses filled with ice and Coca-Cola. The woman stopped short, and stared at their clasped hands. Her eyebrows shot up and her mouth opened, but no words came out. Her eyes went from Janice's face to his, then back.

Janice and Nate released hands, and leaned back, though

Nate would have happily held hands until closing. To hell with the pizza.

Pursing her lips and shaking her head, the cashier lowered the tray to the Formica tabletop between them, letting it clatter the last few inches with some Coke spilling out of each glass.

"Well, that shattered the mood, don't you think?" Janice said with a wry smile.

J anice's mother arrived ten minutes later. Janice, her back to the door, never saw her coming. She and Nate were into their third slices of pizza, the dough soft and chewy, and the cheese flavored with garlic and oregano.

They'd restored the previously shattered mood, holding hands with one hand, and eating pizza with the other. Nate was describing the dizzying culture change when his family moved from Yazoo City, Mississippi, to here in Lynn, Massachusetts. Janice thought she could listen to him all night.

"So this is what you needed the car for today?" her mother demanded.

Janice sat bolt upright. "Mom, what are you doing here?"

Her mother crossed her arms. She was a hefty woman, forty-five years old but with aging lines and crow's feet that made her face look more like fifty-five or sixty. Her eyes shot daggers at Janice. "Let's just say I got a phone call from a friend"—she glanced over in the direction of the cashier—"a friend who was concerned my daughter was disgracing the family."

"Well in that case, your friend was wrong," Janice said. "I've done nothing—"

Her mother grabbed Janice by the wrist and squeezed tightly. "Don't you smart-mouth me! You're holding hands with a goddamned... *with a goddamned Negro*! In public! What the hell is the matter with you!"

"Mother," Janice said, wincing as the pain shot up from her wrist to her elbow, "This is Nate. He helped me out yesterday when a boy... when a boy thought he could grope me and get away with it."

"So what are you doing, *rewarding* him?"

"No, I'm not rewarding him at all. By being with me, he's rewarding *me*," Janice said. "He's a nicer person, a better human being, and a whole lot more interesting than any boyfriend I ever had."

Her mother just stared in shock. "Just wait until your father hears about this."

The words hung in the air, heavy and somber.

"May I say something?" the cashier asked.

Janice's mother nodded. "Go ahead. She ain't listening to me."

"I'm sure you think this is none of my business," the cashier said, "but I'm going to tell you the God's honest truth, and if you listen to me, you might thank me some day." She nodded, as if agreeing with herself. "I sure hope all you've done with this Negro is hold his hand, like I seen you doing. If so, it's not too late. But you best break this off before you ruin your life and break your parents' hearts. Because once this boy"—she pointed at Nate—"once he touches you, you're ruined. You hear me? Ruined! Ain't no self-respecting white boy ever going to want to go anywhere near you ever again. You think about that, Missy!"

"Don't you *dare* talk about Nate that way!" Janice said.

"You're right," the cashier said. "She ain't listening."

"You two," Janice's mother said, pointing at the two teenagers, "You finish up in here. I'll be outside. I want you out there in five minutes." She glared at Nate. "You're not getting alone in a car with my daughter. I'll drive you both home."

After the two adults left,. Janice and Nate stared at each other.

"I'm sorry," they both said, in unison, then gave a mournful snort.

"They can't keep us apart forever," Janice said, taking Nate's hand.

"You mean that?" Nate asked.

"Absolutely!"

"Well, in that case, I don't want to make things any more difficult than they're going to be anyway, but..."

"What?"

"Will you go with me to the prom?" Nate asked.

Janice beamed. "I'll need to sneak out."

"Don't do it if you'll get into too much trouble."

"Can you imagine the looks on everyone's faces?" Janice asked.

"I only care about the look on your face."

The words pierced Janice to her heart. She almost asked him where he'd been all her life, but she knew the answer. For the last three years, he'd been there waiting. Waiting for her to open her eyes.

A tear leaked down her face as she caressed his hand.

"It's a date."

DRUMBEATS
KEVIN J. ANDERSON AND NEIL PEART

Kevin J. Anderson, who is a New York Times *bestselling author of more than 140 novels, regularly appears in Pulphouse with a fresh, new Dan Shamble, Zombie P.I. Adventure. But when I was conjuring up the theme for this particular volume, one of my favorite Anderson stories of all time would not leave me alone. "Drumbeats," which Anderson co-authored with the late Neil Peart, best known as the lyricist and drummer for the rock trio Rush.*

It represents the first collaborative writing between the two that would eventually lead to many stories and novels, among other projects.

It was originally published in Shock Rock II, *edited by Jeff Gelb in 1994. I was thrilled to bring this tale of a drummer in search of an oh-so-magical drum to Pulphouse readers, and now again in this anthology.*

Perhaps, like me, you will feel the uncanny and relentless beat of the story resonate and throb within you.

DRUMBEATS

KEVIN J. ANDERSON AND NEIL PEART

After nine months of touring across North America—with hotel suites and elaborate dinners and clean sheets every day—it felt good to be hot and dirty, muscles straining not for the benefit of any screaming audience, but just to get to the next village up the dusty road, where none of the natives recognized Danny Imbro or knew his name. To them, he was just another White Man, an exotic object of awe for little children, a target of scorn for drunken soldiers at border checkpoints.

Bicycling through Africa was about the furthest thing from a rock concert tour that Danny could imagine—which was why he did it, after promoting the latest Blitzkrieg album and performing each song until the tracks were worn smooth in his head. This cleared his mind, gave him a sense of balance, perspective.

The other members of Blitzkrieg did their own thing during the group's break months. Phil, whom they called the "music machine" because he couldn't stop writing music, spent his relaxation time cranking out film scores for Hollywood; Reggie caught up on his reading, soaking up grocery bags full of political thrillers and mysteries; Shane turned into a vegetable on Maui. But Danny Imbro took his expensive-but-battered bicycle and bummed around West Africa. The others thought it strangely appropriate that the band's drummer would go off hunting for tribal rhythms.

Late in the afternoon on the sixth day of his ride through Cameroon, Danny stopped in a large open market and bus depot in the town of Garoua. The marketplace was a line of mud-brick kiosks and chophouses, the air filled with the smell of baked dust and stones, hot oil and frying beignets. Abandoned cars squatted by the roadside, stripped clean but unblemished by corrosion in the dry air. Groups of men and children in long blouses like nightshirts idled their time away on the street corners.

Wives and daughters appeared on the road with their buckets, going to fetch water from the well on the other side of the marketplace. They wore bright-colored *pagnes* and kerchiefs, covering their traditionally naked breasts with T-shirts or castoff Western blouses, since the government in the capital city of Yaounde had forbidden women from going topless.

Behind one kiosk in the shade sat a pan holding several bottles of Coca-Cola, Fanta, and ginger ale, cooling in water. Some vendors sold a thin stew of bony fish chunks over gritty rice, others sold *fufu*, a dough-like paste of pounded yams to be dipped into a sauce of meat and okra. Bread merchants stacked their long *baguettes* like dry firewood.

Danny used the back of his hand to smear sweat-caked dust off his forehead, then removed the bandanna he wore under his helmet to keep the sweat out of his eyes. With streaks of white skin peeking through the layer of grit around his eyes, he probably looked like some strange lemur.

In halting French, he began haggling with a wiry boy to buy a bottle of water. Hiding behind his kiosk, the boy demanded 800 francs for the water, an outrageous price. While Danny attempted to bargain it down, he saw the gaunt, grayish-skinned man walking through the marketplace like a wind-up toy running down.

The man was playing a drum.

The boy cringed and looked away. Danny kept staring. The crowd seemed to shrink away from the strange man as he wandered among them, continuing his incessant beat. He wore his hair long and unruly, which in itself was unusual among the close-cropped Africans. In the equatorial heat, the long stained overcoat he wore must have heated his body like a furnace, but the man did not seem to notice. His eyes were focused on some invisible distance.

"*Huit-cent francs,*" the boy insisted on his price, holding the lukewarm bottle of water just out of Danny's reach.

The staggering man walked closer, tapping a slow monotonous beat on the small cylindrical drum under his arm. He did not change his tempo, but continued to play as if his life depended on it. Danny saw that the man's fingers and wrists were wrapped with scraps of hide; even so, he had beaten his fingertips bloody.

Danny stood transfixed. He had heard tribal musicians play all manner of percussion instruments, from hollowed tree trunks, to rusted metal cans, to beautifully carved *djembe* drums with goat-skin drumheads—but he had never heard a tone so rich and sweet, with such an odd echoey quality as this strange African drum.

In the studio, he had messed around with drum synthesizers and reverbs and the new technology designed to turn computer hackers into musicians. But this drum sounded different, solid and pure, and it hooked him through the heart, hypnotizing him. It distracted him entirely from the unpleasant appearance of its bearer.

"What is that?" he asked.

"*Sept-cent francs,*" the boy insisted in a nervous whisper, dropping his price to 700 and pushing the water closer.

Danny walked in front of the staggering man, smiling broadly enough to show the grit between his teeth, and listened to the tapping drumbeat. The drummer turned his gaze to Danny and stared through him. The pupils of his eyes were like two gaping bullet wounds through his skull. Danny took a step backward, but found himself moving to the beat. The drummer faced him, finding his audience. Danny tried to place the rhythm, to burn it into his mind—something this mesmerizing simply had to be included in a new Blitzkrieg song.

Danny looked at the cylindrical drum, trying to determine what might be causing its odd double-resonance—a thin inner membrane, perhaps? He saw nothing but elaborate carvings on the sweat polished wood, and a drumhead with a smooth, dark brown coloration. He knew the Africans used all kinds of skin for their drumheads, and he couldn't begin to guess what this was.

He mimed a question to the drummer, then asked, "*Est-ce-que je peux l'essayer?*" May I try it?

The gaunt man said nothing, but held out the drum near

enough for Danny to touch it without interrupting his obsessive rhythm. His overcoat flapped open, and the hot stench of decay made Danny stagger backward, but he held his ground, reaching for the drum.

Danny ran his fingers over the smooth drumskin, then tapped with his fingers. The deep sound resonated with a beat of its own, like a heartbeat. It delighted him. "For sale? *Est-ce-que c'est a vendre?*" He took out a thousand francs as a starting point, although if water alone cost 800 francs here, this drum was worth much, much more.

The man snatched the drum away and clutched it to his chest, shaking his head vigorously. His drumming hand continued its unrelenting beat.

Danny took out two thousand francs, then was disappointed to see not the slightest change of expression on the odd drummer's face. "Okay, then, where was the drum made? Where can I get another one? *Où est-ce qu'on peut trouver un autre comme ça?*" He put most of the money back into his pack, keeping 200 francs out. Danny stuffed the money into the fist of the drummer; the man's hand seemed to be made of petrified wood. "*Où?*"

The man scowled, then gestured behind him, toward the Mandara Mountains along Cameroon's border with Nigeria. "*Kabas.*"

He turned and staggered away, still tapping on his drum as if to mark his footsteps. Danny watched him go, then returned to the kiosk, unfolding the map from his pack. "Where is this Kabas? Is it a place? *C'est un village?*"

"*Huit-cent francs,*" the boy said, offering the water again at his original 800 franc price.

Danny bought the water, and the boy gave him directions.

He spent the night in a Garouan hotel that made Motel 6 look like Caesar's Palace. Anxious to be on his way to find his own new drum, Danny roused a local vendor and cajoled him into preparing a quick omelet for breakfast. He took a sip from his 800-franc bottle of water, saving the rest for the long bike ride, then pedaled off into the stirring sounds of early morning.

As Danny left Garoua on the main road, heading toward the mountains, savanna and thorn trees stretched away under a crystal sky. A pair of doves bathed in the dust of the road ahead, but as he rode toward them, they flew up into the last of the trees with a *chuk-chuk* of alarm and a flash of white tail feathers. Smoke from grassfires on the plains tainted the air.

How different it was to be riding through a landscape, he thought—with no walls or windows between his senses and the world—rather than just riding by it. Danny felt the road under his thin wheels, the sun, the wind on his body. It made a strange place less exotic, yet it became infinitely more real.

The road out of Garoua was a wide boulevard that turned into a smaller road heading north. With his bicycle tires humming and crunching on the irregular pavement, Danny passed a few ragged cotton fields, then entered the plains of dry, yellow grass and thorny scrub, everywhere studded with boulders and sculpted anthills. By 7:30 in the morning, a hot breeze rose, carrying a honeysuckle-like perfume. Everything vibrated with heat.

Within an hour the road grew worse, but Danny kept his pace, taking deep breaths in the trancelike state that kept the horizon moving closer. Drums. Kabas. Long rides helped him clear his head, but he found he had to concentrate to steer around the worst ruts and the biggest stones.

Great columns of stone appeared above the hills to east and west. One was pyramid-shaped, one a huge rounded breast, yet another a great stone phallus. Danny had seen photographs of these "inselberg" formations caused by volcanoes that had eroded over the eons, leaving behind vertical cores of lava.

Erosion had struck the road here, too, turning it into a heaving washboard, which then veered left into a trough between tumbled boulders and up through a gauntlet of thorn trees. Danny stopped for another drink of water, another glance at the map. The water boy at the kiosk had marked the location of Kabas with his fingernail, but it was not printed on the map.

After Danny had climbed uphill for an hour, the beaten path became no more than a worn trail, forcing him to squeeze between walls of thorns and dry millet stalks. The squadrons of hovering dragonflies were harmless, but the hordes of tiny flies circling his face were maddening, and he couldn't pedal fast enough to escape them.

It was nearly noon, the sun reflecting straight up from the dry earth, and the little shade cast by the scattered trees dwindled to a small circle around the trunks. "Where the hell am I going?" he said to the sky.

But in his head he kept hearing the odd, potent beat resonating from the bizarre drum he had seen in the Garoua marketplace. He recalled the grayish, shambling man who had never once stopped tapping on his drum, even though his fingers bled. No matter how bad the road got, Danny thought, he would keep going. He'd never been so intrigued by a drumbeat before, and he never left things half finished.

Danny Imbro was a goal-oriented person. The other members of Blitzkrieg razzed him about it, that once he made up his mind to do something, he plowed ahead, defying all common sense. Back in school, he had made up his mind to be a drummer. He had hammered away at just about every object in sight with his fingertips, pencils, silverware, anything that made noise. He kept at it until he drove everyone else around him nuts, and somewhere along the line he became good.

Now people stood at the chain-link fences behind concert halls and applauded whenever he walked from the backstage dressing rooms out to the tour buses—as if he were somehow doing a better job of walking than any of them had ever seen before.

Up ahead, an enormous buttress-tree, a gnarled and twisted pair of trunks hung with cable-thick vines, cast a wide patch of shade. Beneath the tree, watching him approach, sat a small boy.

The boy leaped to his feet, as if he had been waiting for Danny. Shirtless and dusty, he held a hooklike withered arm against his chest; but his grin was completely disarming. "*Je suis guide?*" the boy called.

Relief stifled Danny's laugh. He nodded vigorously. "*Oui!*" Yes, he could certainly use a guide right about now. "*Je cherche Kabas—village des tambours*. The village of drums."

The smiling boy danced around like a goat, jumping from rock to rock. He was pleasant-faced and healthy looking, except for the crippled arm; his skin was very dark but his eyes had a slight Asian cast. He chattered in a high voice, a mixture of French and native dialect. Danny caught enough to understand that the boy's name was Anatole.

Before the boy led him on, though, Danny dismounted, leaning his bicycle against a boulder, and unzipped his pack to take out the raisins, peanuts, and the dry remains of a baguette. Anatole watched him with wide eyes, and Danny gave him a handful of raisins, which the boy wolfed down. Small flies whined around their faces as they ate. Danny answered the boy's incessant questions with as few words as possible: did he come from America, did black boys live there, why was he visiting Cameroon?

The short rest sank its soporific claws into him, but Danny decided not to give in. An afternoon siesta made a lot of sense, but now that he had his own personal guide to the village, he made it his goal not to stop again until they reached Kabas. "Okay?" Danny raised his eyebrows and struggled to his feet.

Anatole sprang out from the shade and fetched Danny's bike for him, struggling with one arm to keep it upright. After several trips to Africa, Danny had seen plenty of withered limbs, caused by childhood diseases, accidents, and bungled inoculations. Out here in the wilder areas, such problems were even more prevalent, and he wondered how Anatole managed to survive; acting as a "guide" for the rare travelers would hardly suffice.

Danny pulled out a hundred francs—an eighth of what he had paid for one bottle of water—and handed it to the boy, who looked as if he had just been handed the crown jewels. Danny figured he had probably made a friend for life.

Anatole trotted ahead, gesturing with his good arm. Danny pedaled after him.

The narrow valley captured a smear of greenness in the dry hills, with a cluster of mango trees, guava trees, and strange baobabs with eight-foot-thick trunks. Playing the knowledgeable tour guide, Anatole explained that the local women used the baobab fruits for baby formula if their breast milk failed. The villagers used another tree to manufacture an insect repellent.

The houses of Kabas blended into the landscape, because they were of the landscape—stones and branches and grass. The walls were made of dry mud, laid on a handful at a time, and the roofs were thatched into cones. Tiny pink and white stones studded the mud, sparkling like quartz in the sun.

At first the place looked deserted, but then an ancient man emerged from a turret-shaped hut. An enormous cutlass dangled from his waist, although the shrunken man looked as if it might take him an hour just to lift the blade. Anatole shouted something, then gestured for Danny to follow him. The great cutlass swayed against the old man's unsteady knees as he bowed slightly—or stooped—and greeted Danny in formal, unpracticed French. *"Bonsoir!"*

"Makonya," Danny said, remembering the local greeting from Garoua. He walked his bike in among the round and square buildings. A few chickens scratched in the dirt, and a pair of black-and-brown goats nosed between the huts. A sinewy, long-limbed old woman wearing only a loincloth tended a fire. He immediately started looking for the special drums, but saw none.

Within the village, a high-walled courtyard enclosed two round huts. Gravel covered the open area between them, roofed over with a network of serpent-shaped sticks supporting grass mats. This seemed to be the chief's compound. Anatole held Danny's arm and dragged him forward.

Inside the wall, a white-robed figure reclined in a canvas chair under an acacia tree. His handsome features had a North African cast, thin lips over white teeth, and a rakish mustache. His aristocratic head was wrapped in a red-and-white checked scarf, and even in repose he was obviously tall. He looked every bit the romantic desert prince, like Rudolf Valentino in The Sheik. After greeting Danny in both French and the local language, the chief gestured for his visitor to sit beside him.

Before Danny could move, two other boys appeared carrying a rolled-up mat of woven grass, which they spread out for him. Anatole scolded them for horning in on his customer, but the two boys cuffed him and ignored his protests. Then the chief shouted at them all for disturbing his peace and drove the boys away. Danny watched them kicking Anatole as they scampered away from the chief, and he felt for his new friend, angry at how tough people picked on weaker ones the world over.

He sat cross-legged on the mat, and it took him only a moment to begin reveling in the moment of relaxation. No cars or trucks disturbed the peace. He was miles from the nearest electricity, or glass window, or airplane. He sat looking up into the leaves of the acacia, listening to the quiet buzz of the villagers, and thought, "I'm living in a National Geographic documentary!"

Anatole stole back into the compound, bearing two bottles of warm Mirinda orange soda, which he gave to Danny and the chief. Other boys gathered under the tree, glaring at Anatole, then looking at Danny with ill-concealed awe.

After several moments of polite smiling and nodding, Danny asked the chief if all the boys were his children. Anatole assisted in the unnecessary translation.

"*Oui*," the chief said, patting his chest proudly. He claimed to have fathered 31 sons, which made Danny wonder if the women in the village found it politic to routinely claim the chief as the father of their babies. As with all remote African villages, though, many children died of various sicknesses. Just a week earlier, one of the babies had succumbed to a terrible fever, the chief said.

The chief asked Danny the usual questions about his country, whether any black men lived there, why had he visited Cameroon; then he insisted that Danny eat dinner with them. The women would prepare the village's specialty of chicken in peanut sauce.

Hearing this, the old sentry emerged with his cutlass, smiled widely at Danny, then turned around the side wall. The squawking of a terrified chicken erupted in the sleepy afternoon air, the sounds of a scuffle, and then the squawking stopped.

Finally, Danny asked the question that had brought him to Kabas in the first place. "*Moi, je suis musicien; je cherche les tambours speciaux.*" He mimed rapping on a small drum, then turned to Anatole for assistance.

The chief sat up startled, then nodded. He hammered on the air, mimicking drum playing, as if to make sure. Danny nodded. The chief clapped his hands and gestured for Anatole to take Danny somewhere. The boy pulled Danny to his feet and, surrounded by other chattering boys, dragged him back out of the walled courtyard. Danny managed to turn around and bow to the chief.

After trooping up a stair-like terrace of rock, they entered the courtyard of another homestead. The main shelter was made of hand-shaped blocks with a flat roof of corrugated metal. Anatole explained that this was the home of the local *sorcier*, or wizard.

Anatole called out, then gestured for Danny to follow through the low doorway. Inside the hut, the walls were hung with evidence of the *sorcier's* trade—odd bits of metal, small carvings, bundles of fur and feathers, mortars full of powders and herbs, clay urns for water and millet beer, smooth skins curing from the roof poles. And drums.

"*Tambours!*" Anatole said, spreading his hands wide.

Judging from the craftsman's tools around the hut, the *sorcier* made the village's drums as well as stored them. Danny saw several small gourd drums, larger log drums, and hollow cylinders of every size, all intricately carved with serpentine symbols, circles feeding into spirals, lines tangled into knots.

Danny reached out to touch one—then the *sorcier* himself stood up from the shadows near the far wall. Danny bit off a startled cry as the lithe old man glided forward. The *sorcier* was tall and rangy, but his skin was a battleground of wrinkles, as if someone had clumsily fashioned him out of *papier maché*.

"Pardon," Danny said. The wrinkled man had been sitting on a low stool, putting the finishing touches to a new drum.

Fixing his eyes on his visitor, the *sorcier* withdrew a medium-sized drum from a niche in the wall. Closing his eyes, he tapped on it. The mud walls of the hut reverberated with the hollow vibration, an earthy, primal beat that resonated in

Danny's bones. Danny grinned with awe. Yes! The gaunt man's drum had not been a fluke. The drums of Kabas had some special construction that caused this hypnotic tone.

Danny reached out tentatively. The wrinkled man gave him an appraising look, then extended the drum enough for Danny to strike it. He tapped a few tentative beats, and laughed out loud when the instrument rewarded him with the same rich sound.

The *sorcier* turned away, taking the drum with him and returning it to its niche in the wall. In two flowing strides, the wrinkled man went to his stool in the shadows, picking up the drum he had been fashioning, moving it into the crack of light that seeped through the windows. Pointing, he spoke in a staccato dialect, which Anatole translated into pidgin French.

The *sorcier* is finishing a new drum today, Anatole said. Perhaps they would play it this evening, an initiation. The chief's baby son would have enjoyed that. From the baby's body, the *sorcier* had been able to salvage only enough skin to make this one small drum.

"What?" Danny said, looking down at the deep brown skin covering the top of the drum.

Anatole explained, as if it was the most ordinary thing in the world, that whenever one of the chief's many sons died, the *sorcier* used his skin to make one of Kabas's special drums. It had always been done.

Danny wrestled with that for a moment. On his first trip to Africa five years earlier, he had learned the wrenching truth of how different these cultures were.

"Why?" he finally asked. *"Pourquoi?"*

He had seen other drums made entirely of human skin taken from slain enemies, fashioned in the shape of stunted bodies with gaping mouths; when tapped a hollow sound came from the effigy's mouths. He knew that trying to impose his Western moral framework on the inhabitants of an alien land was hopeless. I'm sorry, sir, but you'll have to check your preconceptions at the door, he thought jokingly to himself.

"*Magique.*" Anatole's eyes showed a flash of fear—fear born of respect for great power, rather than paranoia or panic. With the magic drums of Kabas, the chief could conquer any man, steal his heartbeat. It was old magic, a technique the village wizards had discovered long before the French had come to Cameroon, and before them the Germans. Kabas had been isolated, and at peace for longer than the memories of the oldest people in the village. Because of the drums. Anatole smiled, proud of his story, and Danny restrained an urge to pat him on the head.

Trying not to let his disbelief show, Danny nodded deeply to the *sorcier*. "*Merci,*" he said. As Anatole led him back out to the courtyard, the *sorcier* returned to his work on the small drum.

Danny wondered if he should have tried to buy one of the drums from the wrinkled man. Did he believe the story about using human skins? Probably. Why would Anatole lie?

As they left the *sorcier's* homestead to begin the trek back to the village, he looked westward across the jagged landscape of inselbergs. At sunset, the air filled with hundreds of kites, their wings rigid, circling high on the last thermals. Like leaves before the wind, the birds came spiraling down to disappear into the trees, filling them with the invisible flapping of wings.

When they reached the main village again, Danny saw that the women had returned from their labor in the nearby fields. He was familiar with the African tradition of sending the women and children out for backbreaking labor while the men lounged in the shade and talked "business."

The numerous sons of the chief and other adults gathered inside the courtyard near the fire, which the old sinewy woman had stoked into a larger blaze. Other men emerged, and Danny wondered where they had been hiding all afternoon. Out hunting? If so, they had nothing to show for their efforts. Anatole directed Danny to sit on a mat beside the chief, and everyone smiled vigorously at each other, the villagers exchanging the call-and-response litany of ritual greetings, which could go on for several minutes.

The old woman served the chief first, then the honored guest. She placed a brown yam like a baked potato on the mat in front of him, miming that it was hot. Danny took a cautious bite; the yam was pungent and turned to paste in his mouth. Then the woman reappeared with the promised chicken in peanut sauce. They ate quietly in a circle around the fire, ignoring each other, as red shadows flickered across their faces.

Listening to the sounds of eating, as well as the simmering evening hush of the West African hills, Danny felt the emptiness like a peaceful vacuum, draining away stress and loud noises and hectic schedules. After too many head-pounding tours and adrenaline-crazed performances, Danny was convinced he had forgotten how to sit quietly, how to slow down. After one rough segment of the last Blitzkrieg tour, he had taken a few days to go camping in the mountains; he recalled pacing in vigorous circles around the picnic table, muttering to himself that he was relaxing as fast as he could! Calming down was an acquired skill, he felt, and there was no better teacher than Africa.

After the meal, heads turned in the firelight, and Danny looked up to see the *sorcier* enter the chief's compound. The wrinkled man cradled several of his mystical drums. He placed one of the drums in front of the chief, then set the others on an empty spot on the ground. He squatted behind one drum, thrusting his long, lean legs up and to the side like the wings of a vulture.

Danny perked up. "A concert?" He turned to Anatole, who spoke rapidly to the *sorcier*. The wrinkled man looked skeptically at Danny, then shrugged. He picked up one of the extra drums and ceremoniously extended it to Danny.

Danny couldn't stop smiling. He took the drum and looked at it. The coffee-colored skin felt smooth and velvety as he touched it. A shiver went up his spine as he tapped the drumhead. Making music from human skin. He forced his instinctive revulsion back into the gray static of his mind, the place where he stored things "to think about later." For now, he had the drum in his hands.

The chief thumped out a few beats, then stopped. The *sorcier* mimicked them, and glanced toward Danny. "Jam session!" he muttered under his breath, then repeated the sequence easily and cleanly, but added a quick, complicated flourish to the end.

The chief raised his eyebrows, followed suit with the beat, and made it more complicated still. The *sorcier* flowed into his part, and Danny joined in with another counterpoint. It reminded him of the Dueling Banjos sequence from Deliverance.

The echoing, rich tone of the drum made his fingers warm and tingly, but he allowed himself to be swallowed up in the mystic rhythms, the primal pounding out in the middle of the

African wilderness. The other night noises vanished around him, the smoke from the fire rose straight up, and the light centered into a pinpoint of his concentration.

Using his bare fingers—sticks would only interrupt the magical contact between himself and the drum—Danny continued weaving into their rhythms, trading points and counterpoints. The beat touched a core of past lives deep within him, an atavistic, pagan intensity, as the three drummers reached into the Pulse of the World. The chief played on; the *sorcier* played on; and Danny let his eyes fade half closed in a rhythmic trance, as they explored the wordless language and hypnotic interplay of rhythm.

Danny became aware of the other boys standing up and swaying, jabbering excitedly and laughing as they danced around him. He deciphered their words as "White man drum!, white man drum!" It was a safe bet they'd never seen a white man play a drum before.

Suddenly the *sorcier* stopped, and within a beat the chief also quit playing. Danny felt wrenched out of the experience, but reluctantly played a concluding figure as well, ending with an emphatic flam. His arms burned from the exertion, sweat dripped down the stubble on his chin. His ears buzzed from the noise. Unable to restrain himself, Danny began laughing with delight.

The *sorcier* said something, which Anatole translated. *"Vous avez l'esprit de batteur."* You have the spirit of a drummer.

With a throbbing hand, Danny squeezed Anatole's bare shoulder and nodded. *"Oui."*

The chief also congratulated him, thanking him for sharing his white man's music with the village. Danny found that ironic, since he had come here to pick up a rich African flavor for his compositions. But Danny could record his impressions in new songs; the village of Kabas had no way of keeping what he had brought to them.

The withered *sorcier* picked up one of the drums at his side, and Danny recognized it as the small drum the old man had been finishing in the dim hut that afternoon. He fixed his deep gaze on Danny for a moment, then handed it to him.

Anatole sat up, alarmed, but bit off a comment he had intended to make. Danny nodded in reassurance and in delight he took the new drum. He held it to his chest and inclined his head deeply to show his appreciation. *"Merci!"*

Anatole took Danny's hand to lead him away from the walled courtyard. The chief clapped his hands and barked something to the other boys, who looked at Anatole with glee before they got up and scurried to the huts for sleeping. Anatole stared nervously at Danny, but Danny didn't understand what had just occurred.

He repeated his thanks, bowing again to the chief and *sorcier*, but the two of them just stared at him. He was reminded of an East African scene: a pair of lions sizing up their prey. He shook his head to clear the morbid thought, and followed Anatole.

In the village proper, one of the round thatched huts had been swept for Danny to sleep in. Outside, his bicycle leaned against a tree, no doubt guarded during the day by the little man with the enormous cutlass. Anatole seemed uneasy, wanting to say something, but afraid.

Trying to comfort him, Danny opened his pack and withdrew a stick of chewing gum for the boy. Anatole boy spoke rapidly, gushing his thanks. Other boys suddenly materialized from the shadows with childish murder in their eyes. They tried to take the gum from Anatole, but he popped it in his mouth and ran off. "Hey!" Danny shouted, but Anatole bolted into the night with the boys chasing after.

Wondering if Anatole was in any real danger, Danny removed the blanket and sleeping bag from his bike, then carried them inside the guest hut. He decided the boy could take care of himself, that he had spent his life as the whipping boy for the other sons of the chief. The thought drained some of the exhilaration from the memory of the evening's performance.

His legs ached after the torturous ride upland from Garoua, and he fantasized briefly about sitting in the Jacuzzi in the capital suite of some five-star hotel. He considered how wonderful it would be to sip on some cold champagne, or a scotch on the rocks.

Instead, he lifted the gift drum, inspecting it. He would find some way to use it on the next album, add a rich African tone to the music. Paul Simon and Peter Gabriel had done it, though the style of Blitzkreig's music was a bit more. . .aggressive.

He would not tell anyone about the human skin, especially the customs officials. He tried without success to decipher the mystical swirling patterns carved into the wood, the inter-woven curves, circles, and knots. It made him dizzy.

Danny closed his eyes and began to play the drum, quietly so as not to disturb the other villagers. But as the sound reached his ears, he snapped his eyes open. The tone from the drum was flat and weak, like a cheap tourist tom-tom, plastic over a coffee can.

He frowned at the gift drum. Where was the rich reverber-ation, the primal pulse of the earth? He tapped again, but

KEVIN J. ANDERSON AND NEIL PEART

heard only an empty and hollow sound, soulless. Danny scowled, wondering if the *sorcier* had ruined the drum by accident, then decided to get rid of it by giving it to the unsuspecting White Man who wouldn't know the difference.

Angry and uneasy, Danny set the African drum next to him; he would try it again in the morning. He could play it for the chief, show him its flat tone. Perhaps they would exchange it. Maybe he would have to buy another one.

He hoped Anatole was all right.

Danny sat down to pull the thorns and prickers from his clothes. The village women had provided him with two plastic basins of water for bathing, one for soaping and scrubbing, the other for rinsing. The warm water felt refreshing on his face, his neck. After stripping off his pungent socks, he rinsed his toes and soles.

The night stillness was hypnotic, and as he spread his sleeping bag and stretched out on it, he felt as if he were seeping into the cloth, into the ground, swallowed up in sleep.

. . .

Anatole woke him up only a few moments later, shaking him and whispering harshly in his ear. Dirt, blood, and bruises covered the boy's wiry body, and his clothes had been torn in a scuffle. He didn't seem to care. He kept shaking Danny.

But it was already too late.

Danny sat up, blinking his eyes. Sharp pains like a bear trap ripped through his chest. A giant hand had wrapped around his torso and would squeeze until his ribs popped free of his spine.

He gasped, opening and closing his mouth, but could not give voice to his agony. He grabbed Anatole's withered arm, but the boy struggled away, searching for something. Black spots swam in his eyes. He tried to breathe, but his chest wouldn't let him. He began slipping, sliding down an endless cliff into blackness.

Anatole finally reached an object on the floor of the hut. He snatched it up with his good hand, tucked it firmly under his withered arm, and began to thump on it.

The drum!

As the boy rapped out a slow steady beat, Danny felt the iron band loosen around his heart. Blood rushed into his head again, and he drew a deep breath. Dizziness continued to swim around him, but the impossible pain receded. He clutched his chest, rubbing his sternum. He uttered a breathy thanks to Anatole.

Had he just suffered a heart attack? Good God, all the fast living had decided to catch up to him while he was out in the middle of nowhere, far from any hope of medical attention!

Then he realized with a chill that the sounds from the gift drum were now rich and echoey, with the unearthly depth he remembered from the other drums. Anatole continued his slow rhythm, and suddenly Danny recognized it. A heartbeat.

What was it the boy had told him inside the sorcier's hut—that the magical drums could steal a man's heartbeat? *"Ton coeur c'est dans ici,"* Anatole said, continuing his drumming. Your heartbeat lives in here now.

Danny remembered the gaunt, shambling man in the marketplace of Garoua, obsessively tapping the drum from Kabas as if his life depended on it, until his hide-wrapped fingers were bloodied. Had that man also escaped his fate in the village, and fled south?

"You had the spirit of a drummer," Anatole said in his pidgin French, "and now the drum has your spirit." As if to emphasize his statement, as if he knew a White Man would be skeptical of such magic, Anatole ceased his rhythm on the drum.

The claws returned to Danny's heart, and the vise in his chest clamped back down. His heart had stopped beating. Heart beats, drumbeats—

The boy stopped only long enough to convince Danny, then started the beat again. He looked with pleading eyes in the shadowy hut. "*Je vais avec toi!*" I go with you. Let me be your heartbeat. From now on.

Leaving his sleeping bag behind, Danny staggered out of the guest hut to his bicycle resting against an acacia tree. The rest of the village was dark and silent, and the next morning they would expect to find him dead and cold on his blankets; and the new drum would have the same resonant quality, the same throbbing of a captured spirit, to add to their collection. The sound of White Man's music for Kabas.

"*Allez!*" Anatole whispered as Danny climbed aboard his bike. Go! What was he supposed to do now? The boy ran in front of him along the narrow track. Danny did not fear navigating the rugged trail by moonlight, with snakes and who-knows-what abroad in the grass, as much as he feared staying in Kabas and being there when the chief and the *sorcier* came to look at his body in the morning, and no doubt to appraise their pale new drum skin.

But how long could Anatole continue his drumming? If the beat stopped for only a moment, Danny would seize up. They would have to take turns sleeping. Would this nightmare continue after he had left the vicinity of the village? Distance had not helped the shambling man in the marketplace in Garoua.

Would this be the rest of his life?

Stricken with panic, Danny nodded to the boy, just wanting to be out of there and not knowing what else to do. Yes, I'll take you with me. What other choice do I have? He pedaled his bike away from Kabas, crunching on the rough dirt path. Anatole jogged in front of him, tapping on the drum.

And tapping.

And tapping.

WHAT REMAINS OF AMERICA

SCOTT EDELMAN

As a number of places online say, Scott Edelman was the editor of
the science fiction magazine Science Fiction Age. He published and
edited the semi-professional magazine Last Wave from 1982 to 1985,
which I sent stories to, but could never sell him a story even though I
tried a bunch.

Other magazines edited by Edelman over the years include Sci-Fi
Universe, Sci-Fi Flix, and Satellite Orbit. He became the editor
of SCI FI Magazine (the official print magazine of The Sci Fi
Channel) in 2002, and has edited the channel's online
magazine Science Fiction Weekly since 2000.

But he did write some for the early years of Pulphouse and now,
his fourth story in this new incarnation should grab you from the
title and take you from there. An amazing look at a horrid future
through the eyes of a great character.

For more information about Scott's writing and editing, go to
www.scottedelman.com

WHAT REMAINS OF AMERICA

SCOTT EDELMAN

After too many treacherous weeks of travel, the old man, spade in hand, was finally ready to begin his long-planned, yet still somehow spontaneous project. The sun was low in the morning sky as he considered the patch of ground he'd been dreaming of, which meant the New York Public Library cast a long, sheltering shadow over where he stood.

A twelve-foot circle should do, he thought. He paced out the border he imagined in the center of Bryant Park, and could see his work as if it were already done.

He began to dig, forcing the tongue of his tool into the hard-packed earth, then swiveling quickly to toss a dry clump of earth behind him. The second spadeful was slightly easier than the first, but not by much. It wasn't long before his wiry arms, which had spent most of a lifetime coercing Idaho soil—save for the most recent unfortunate years which had put that beyond him, beyond all of them—began quivering from his attempt to excavate what millions of feet had compressed.

Millions of feet long gone.

71

The effort, more than he'd had reason to exert lately, made him think about what had been lost when everything changed —but also about how thinking too much was what had brought him here, so many hundreds of miles from home.

Before even an hour had passed, a heart flutter warned he should rest. But the pile of earth he'd removed by then seemed so small, and the pit so shallow—how dare his body rebel that soon! He thrust his spade in the mound he'd made, and went to sit on the running board of the truck he'd pulled near the fountain after driving up the steps which edged the park, something he could not imagine having done during his earlier visit, in the before times, when the city was still a city instead of just a collection of uninhabited buildings and over-grown roads.

Manhattan was quieter than he'd thought it would be when he drove east, even taking into account the changes the world had wrought. The pounding in his ears seemed to be the loudest noise on the island. Bryant Park was empty, which was as he needed it to be, and he'd spotted no other survivors while navigating around less rubble than he'd expected, and dodging potholes which had grown into craters after years of disrepair.

If he'd wished, he could have pretended to be the last man on Earth.

Not even the wind intruded on him that morning. But if there'd been a breeze, it would have found no leaves to rustle nor blades of grass to stir. Life had been almost entirely evicted from the city long before by those fools who thought they knew best, as fools always did. Especially the biggest fool of all, whose name he didn't even want to think.

The grass beneath his feet was brown and detached from

the ground, no longer a lawn hugging the soil, but scattered loosely like clippings on a barbershop floor, back when barber- shops were a thing. The trees, stripped of their bark, had been flattened and were neatly parallel as they lay pointing uptown, almost as if placed there by design.

Winter had been warmer than usual, and he was thankful for that, as he didn't know if he could have made it all the way from Idaho to New York if the country had been blan- keted in snow, the way he remembered it having been the last time he'd been there, when he and his wife, his poor, dear wife, had flown out twenty years earlier to celebrate their twenty-fifth wedding anniversary. That had been the first and would forever be the last time they'd come east together. New York City had been the biggest present he could think of giving her, but as it turned out, she hadn't cared for the place, and he hadn't liked it much either. Cities were not for them. Too big, too busy, too disconnected from the soil.

He wondered what she'd have made of the place now.

He wished she'd had the chance to find out.

But enough remembering—he'd have plenty of time for that on the long drive home.

He pulled himself up with the spade and stood propped against it for a moment before returning to his preparations for what was to come.

He started to dig once more, and with each measured swing of his spade, the mound between the pit and the pickup grew larger. He worked slowly but steadily, for he hoped to complete his task by nightfall. He didn't want to remain on this dead island any longer than needed, so he only rested when his heart ordered him to, a heart which sometimes pounded so wildly he feared it might burst and swell to encompass the city.

Considering the deepening hole before him and the growing pile behind, it occurred to him he could have been mistaken for a gravedigger.

Maybe that's what I am, he thought, smiling grimly. *Maybe.*

As far as death went, he was sure those back home thought *him* dead. Once he'd spontaneously commandeered the truck —because in that instant, it suddenly seemed the right thing, the necessary thing, the only thing to do—they surely thought they'd never see him again. And why wouldn't they think that? For he'd started heading east, where most of the deadliest bombs had dropped those long years ago. But he swore he'd surprise them. He knew the ways of this land better than anyone, knew he'd be able to eke out his survival no matter how those idiots destroyed what lay between.

As he'd traveled, he was in awe before the state of the country, and not in a good way, not in the way one should be in awe, for what he'd discovered proved what he'd feared had been right—that they'd figured out a way to kill almost all the people while leaving the buildings intact.

He looked up at the one beside which he worked, having to shield his eyes, for by then the sun had crept over the roof. As long as the New York Public Library was still whole, that was all that mattered to him now.

As he tossed the last few necessary clumps of earth, he thought of his granddaughter. Out of his once overgrown family tree, she was all family he had left, for the powers that be had pruned it well. Luckily, because of where they lived, because of how they lived, they'd missed the worst of it.

He hoped she wasn't having too much trouble back home

trying to explain his behavior, but figured what neighbors remained knew enough not to bother her much. They'd all thought of him as ornery and irresponsible anyhow even before this, and his theft of his own pickup probably proved it to them.

Theft, he thought angrily, and spat into the circle he'd created.

Taking that truck wasn't stealing. That truck had been *his* before the county seized it after the catastrophe.

That's what we'd come to. A man couldn't even own his own truck. The President would have been surprised to find that letting the missiles fly had pushed America over into communism. But that sociopath would never know—the last president of the United States had probably died in the first moments, or so the old man hoped. He would have deserved it, too, he thought, for killing most of the rest, and for all he'd done to kill democracy even before then.

Some said the President was still alive, flying above the holocaust on a nuclear-powered Air Force One, waiting for the day he could land and resume control. He didn't put much faith in that rumor. But myth or not, he knew a lot of people who were practicing their sharpshooting for when and if that day came.

He didn't need his spade any longer, so he tossed it in the back of the truck. The circle, a dozen feet round and nearly a foot deep, wasn't as wide or as deep as he'd have liked, but it was the best he was capable of.

It didn't look big enough to hold all of America, but would have to do.

He retrieved his rifle from the front seat of his truck and walked around the side toward the library's service entrance.

No carved lions graced those doors—those only stood guard out front. Just as well. He didn't have the stomach for anything noble anymore. They were lies which had no place in this time.

The door was open, and he entered slowly, rifle tight in his hands. A truck, its doors wide, had been backed up to the loading dock. Boxes of books had fallen out and split on the pavement, and shreds of paper were scattered in drifts on the stairs which led inside, the work of vandals who'd come after. He could understand how all that had happened could make some hate books.

He trudged through the debris, and once inside the marble halls, could see scattered signs of violence. Toppled statues. A patch of dried blood smeared along a wall. As he moved deeper, the damage lessened, though. The looters who'd come to the city since the radioactivity level had dropped enough not to kill them instantly—though as he knew and no longer cared, it would kill eventually, and sooner rather than later—had turned back once they realized there was nothing of value here. Not in this world. Who could they have sold anything to? There were a billion times as many books as there were people now, and couldn't be eaten.

He took a wide stairwell to a room he'd visited years before. It seemed silly now, but he'd dragged Marion there during their anniversary visit, forced her to come with him to the room that housed copies of all the nation's telephone books. There was one for each city in the United States, and every person in America who owned a phone well—a landline phone anyway—was listed. Some books were only a few dozen pages long, others inches thick.

Back then, he'd found, in a volume little requested, his own name. Above his, in strict alphabetical order, was his wife's. Finding that page had seemed important then. But now...as far as he was concerned, only one thing was still important.

He walked down the long rows of bookcases until he found the Idaho phone books. There he pulled down the one for his city and flipped through, looking for his name. He came across it quickly, and this time he was the only one with that surname in the book. His wife's name was no longer there.

He tore out the page bearing his name, folded it with great precision, and slid it into a pocket of his overalls.

He tossed the book—printed more than a decade before—in the air and caught it again. It might have been small, but still, it was solid and heavy in his hands.

Down in the shipping room, he found a dolly, loaded high with boxes of books which had never been opened and had been sitting undelivered for years. After removing them, he wheeled the dolly up a series of ramps until he'd returned to the wall of phone books. There were so many of them, many more than he'd remembered, more than he'd thought there'd be, thousands of volumes filled with millions of names. He loaded as many of them as he could, then paused, nodding at the sight of how few shelves he had emptied. It would take him dozens of trips, maybe more. Considering what he'd planned to do, it seemed as if it might be too much. And yet... there was nothing to do but begin.

Once on the street, the dolly protested at being pushed across broken concrete. Its wheels, not having been oiled in decades, creaked loudly. A Chagrin Falls phonebook slid off one of the stacks, bouncing on the uneven ground. He left it where it had fallen, not wanting to lose his momentum. Back in the park, the dolly was difficult to push through the dead grass, so he switched to the other end and pulled it until he reached the pit.

He lifted the books one by one and solemnly called out the city on the each book's cover before dropping it into the hole he'd made. His voice sounded strange to him amid the city's silence. A puff of dust erupted as each volume smacked against the ground. Some of the cities were familiar to him, some he'd never heard of at all. As the books continued to fly through the air, the soft thud of them hitting the dirt was replaced by a slapping sound as each volume landed atop the one thrown a moment before.

He pushed the dolly back inside for a second run, and soon, new books joined the others in the pit. He stepped back and considered the growing pile. He really didn't have to bring them all out here, he knew that. He could even stop now. These would be symbol enough. But then he lifted his head to look at the emptiness around him and knew he must continue.

He returned for another trip, and then another. San Diego joined the pit, and Seattle, and St. Paul. The pile of telephone books, having filled the pit level with the lawn, then rose way above it, towering like a haystack so high he had to fling each new volume far into the air to add them to the top. His entire body trembled from the effort. He'd underestimated the amount of space he'd need, and overestimated his stamina. Would one more load, could one more load, be enough of a symbol?

It would have to be.

He loaded the last of the books—the last he was capable of moving, anyway—onto the dolly slowly. He was savoring his movements carefully this final time, memorizing each motion so he could bring a description of his actions intact to his granddaughter. It was important he remember these moments. The memory was as important, if not more important, than the deed.

Out on 40th Street, he even allowed himself to pause for a moment to admire the Radiator Building before wheeling past and heading into the park. But then he saw—

The driver's side door of his pickup was open.

He threw himself to the ground, taking cover behind the wall of books.

"Who's there?" he shouted. He crawled to one side of the dolly so he could peer out, letting the aim of his rifle drift across the landscape.

No one seemed to be hiding in the piles of trees along the perimeter of the park. He peered back at the library for a moment, but no—the windows were empty. He began to rise, and then dropped down again when he heard a scratching sound coming from the inside the cabin of his truck. The engine turned over once and then sparked to life. He patted at his pocket and found his keys still there.

The son of a bitch hotwired it! he thought. He peered out and shouted, "Get the Hell out of my truck!"

The only answer was the engine's roar.

Belly to the earth, he crawled to the massive mound of books he'd built so he could find a better shooting angle. He fired a warning shot that plowed into the earth inches from the front fender. A moment later, the truck rocked as the emergency brake was released. A man—bearded, filthy—stuck his head up for an instant to get his bearings as the pickup slowly began to roll forward, but pulled it down quickly before the old man could fire off another shot.

79

"Don't," he shouted. "Just don't—you're not going anywhere with my truck, you son of a bitch! I need it to get home. I'm warning you!"

The truck continued to crawl across the park, and he remained hidden behind the mound, tracking the pickup with the barrel of his gun. Suddenly, the truck picked up speed, and the driver poked his head up into view, slamming the door and spinning the wheel, steering toward an exit.

"If that's how you want to play it," the old man whispered.

He rose from behind his cover, lifted the rifle to one shoulder, and squeezed the trigger. Glass exploded, and the man fell to one side across the front seat. The truck swerved and slammed into a clump of fallen trees.

Raising his rifle, he walked slowly alongside the revving vehicle to the front seat. He opened the door with his free hand to find the man now slumped against the steering wheel. He used his rifle barrel to poke at him, which caused him to tilt toward the opening and fall from the truck cabin.

The man was dead.

The old man couldn't tell much about the thief. He didn't have much of a face left. He wore ragged jeans and a torn shirt, and there was nothing in his pockets which gave away who he had been or where he had come from. He could have been anybody.

He could have been *him*.

He climbed into his truck, trying to ignore the blood on the seat, and shifted into reverse. He backed it by the pit and shut the engine.

He rested his head against the steering wheel and realized he needed to catch his breath. When he'd imagined this trip, he'd hoped it wouldn't have to come to this. He pressed the fingers of his right hand against his left wrist. When his pulse finally slowed, he stared across the park at the fallen man. There was only one thing left to do.

He climbed out of the truck. Taking the man's feet, he dragged the body over to the pile of phone books, unsuccessfully trying to ignore the red trail he left behind. He shoved books left and right until there was a space cleared on the mound where he could carefully wedge the body. He retrieved the remaining phonebooks he'd last been wheeling out and used them to cover the corpse, then walked back along the path he'd taken to and from the library, collecting those which had fallen during each trip, and added those to the pile as well.

The sun was beginning to set behind the empty towers at his back when he pulled a can from his truck and circled the base of the mound, pouring gasoline along the books at the outer edges. He pulled a lighter from his pocket, his father's lighter. He remembered the day the old man had given it to him. He closed his eyes, and touched it to his lips. With eyes still shut, he flicked it alive, and for a moment let the brightness seep through his damp lids.

Then he opened his eyes again, and kneeling, held the lighter to the nearest gas-soaked book.

Its cover flamed, blackening pages curling back. He stepped away, his breath ragged in his throat. For a moment, it looked as if the flames wouldn't spread, but an instant later, fire leapt to the next book, and then jumped again and again until a bright ring of flame had sprouted about base of the mound. The paper writhed and fell to embers, burning away Boston, Anchorage, and Portland. Snarling and spitting, the flames began to arc their way up the curve of the pile. The covers, filled with smiling faces and rainbows and cool green landscapes, turned to ash, revealing page after endless page of names which were swallowed up by the unforgiving fire which soared tall into the approaching night.

The heat dried the tears on the old man's face as quickly as they fell.

I've seen too many clouds of smoke and fire, he thought. *But it's right there should be one more.*

When the smell of burning flesh reached his nostrils, he wanted to turn away, but forced himself to watch. He settled on the hood of his truck as pages followed people into dust and beyond, and cried until he fell asleep, the rifle cradled in his lap.

He was still asleep when the sun rose, the rifle held tight in his hands as he lay back on the windshield. The morning sun warm on his face, he dreamt of an eternal cloud of flame.

He woke with a cry.

He looked blankly at the mound of ashes as if seeing it for the first time. But then he remembered. He remembered it all. He remembered his wife.

At least you went before this, he thought. *I wouldn't want you to have seen this.*

He placed the rifle down on the hood and nodded.

He retrieved an empty peanut butter jar from the glove compartment of his truck, then knelt by the remains of the fire and packed it as full as he could with what remained of America. He twisted the lid tight. He stayed on his knees, and with his eyes closed, said a silent prayer.

Then, after placing the jar beside him on a bloodstain he wished he hadn't had to make, he left the empty city and drove across an empty country toward home.

THE HENCHMAN IS HURLED OFF THE CATWALK

ADAM-TROY CASTRO

Seasoned professional Adam-Troy Castro sold Kris and me stories for the very first incarnations of the different Pulphouse magazines.

I love the format of this very innovative story. Only a real professional could pull this off.

You can find a lot more information about Adam-Troy's work and his amazing and long career at his website https://www.adamtroycastro.com/

THE HENCHMAN IS HURLED OFF THE CATWALK

ADAM-TROY CASTRO

S omething's seriously wrong with the angle here.

This, Hennessy thinks, makes no sense at all.

———

H e's looking up at the vast dome of the installation's false ceiling, that curved space that somehow always reminded him of a cathedral, with that barely visible seam marking the spot where the two halves part to admit helicopters and other VTOL aircraft, and crossing it the diagonal slash of the walkway where a dozen of his friends are battling that figure in black, and for this moment at least it doesn't make any sense at all, because he has not realized that he's falling looking up at his flailing legs and cannot discern how they're supported by a solid floor, as they should be. This is a pure exercise in geometry failing to gel, and if anybody happened to take a photo of his face right now it would therefore not betray terror but the irritation we all feel when the dynamics of the world fail to line up. Hennessy is briefly reminded of a tile pattern the boss once used for the floor of the cafeteria, black squares alternating with white squares in the same juxtaposition that has worked for floor tiles since time immemorial, and for some reason it had played havoc with the eyes, its actual distance at any time popping in and out of focus, in a manner that had made Hennessy not want to look at it. It had been an unintended result and the boss had ordered the tiles changed to a more neutral homogenous gray. The catwalk Hennessy's looking up at, through the gap in his trailing legs, feels like a similar optical illusion, as if it's really up there and he's down here looking at it, that would mean he was falling headfirst to his death on the jagged rocks far below, the part of the volcanic crater that the boss had ordered left natural. That's clearly impossible because life is Hennessy's movie and it would not subject him to a death like this, except, look, the catwalk is farther away now than it was at the fraction of a second ago when this train of thought began, and he has been left flailing not just in fact but also for any better explanations.

———

In the last millisecond of denial before he accepts that he is falling to his death Hennessy sees the figure in black do something blurred by speed and send another of the installation's guardians, Lopez, over the railing and following Hennessy's own trajectory. Unlike Hennessy, who is plummeting backward and looking up, Lopez is plummeting face first and looking down, his eyes little black dots in wider white circles, his mouth an off-center black rhombus inhabited by the pink worm that is his protesting tongue. Lopez's limbs are all bent at right angles, the pinwheeling legs following one axis and the pinwheeling arms following another, and for an instant while looking up at him Hennessy recognizes what he's looking at as a fairly impressive rendering of a swastika, and this amuses him for some reason, though he doesn't actually laugh out loud. One reason he doesn't is that the spectacle of Lopez's falling body gives him leave to extrapolate the man's predicament to his own, and he thinks, *Oh, shit, I am falling*, and from there the natural conclusion, *I'm gonna die*, and though his heart gives a wholly unpleasant jolt the epiphany brings not terror, but irritation. That son of a bitch the figure in black has killed him, and that's not supposed to happen to Hennessy, the center of the universe, the viewpoint character who is the star of the mind-movie he's been living all his life. It doesn't even make sense that it has happened, because in the last twenty-four hours the boss has both trapped the interloper in an exploding warehouse and thrown him out the hatch of an airplane without a parachute, and sheer decency would have required the man to just die as would have been only reasonable who had those things done to him, instead of somehow soldiering on and showing up twenty minutes before zero hour to start setting off explosions and throwing guys off catwalks. That's not the way things are supposed to work. That's not the universe as Hennessy understands it. That is not the real-world physics that Hennessy and Lopez (and whoops, farther up, Wu, joining the storm of plummeting bodies) are experiencing right now, and the sudden sound of machine gun fire from one of the upper levels, targeting the figure in black to try to put an end to this nonsense, is not sufficient comfort.

The dominant theme of Hennessy's indignance is not *that son of a bitch* killed *me*, but *that son of a bitch killed me*. It's not the crime, it's the perspective. And it turns out to be true, what they say about life flashing before your eyes. Hennessy remembers who he is. He grew up poor as dirt, barefoot in ragged pants and spending as much time away from his family's shack as possible, mostly because his father was an abusive son of a bitch and his mother was a beaten-down rag whose regard for their shared son was mostly relief that the union had produced a being who could save her some pain by functioning, sometimes, as substitute target. By the time he was ten he was a sneak thief, and by the time he was twelve he was a drug runner, knifing his first guy at fourteen, and honestly, he still looks on those days with a deep and abiding sense of nostalgia, because while it was brutal and soul-destroying and he spent more time hungry that anybody would ever want, it had also been fun, not like this latest gig he got through his pal Rocco, of patrolling this vast complex and hoping his shift would be over before it next occurred to the boss to gather everybody together in formation, to listen to one of his megalomaniacal rants. (And, oh God, those are deadly.) Hennessy has a girlfriend now, Teresa; and sure, they even have a son together, little Emilio; and yes, because he's not such a bad guy he tries to be a better dad than his dad was, and mostly pulls it off, and yes, the job pays several decimal points higher than anything he did while dodging the enforcers of rival gangs on narrow little shit-smelling streets, but it's regimented, more like being in the army than he imagined, and shit, the last thing he'd ever wanted to do was join the army. He's mostly been doing it because the pay is through the roof and because he's never imagined that the boss's plans —which always struck him as unlikely—would ever come to fruition. Still, you make sacrifices when you have a family to support. You put on your uniform, you carry your weapon, you patrol the catwalks, you protect your boss and shudder when the guy in black is tossed out the airplane. At night you return to company housing, have a nice dinner with Teresa, talk about taking all the money you're banking and move to some little community somewhere, where you can get a job that never entails being shot at. You dare to think you'll get through this. That's what you do, if you're a guy like Hennessy. And then the guy in black rappels in and starts tossing people hither and yon, and it's all over. Honestly. He'll be dead the second he hits the rocks, and it matters not that the same is true of all his coworkers, if that countdown to the self-destruct sequence is to be believed. His end is the one that completely shakes his understanding of the universe, and it's so goddamned unfair that Hennessy can't take it.

———

Wind resistance begins to turn Hennessy's plummeting form, relieving him of any further eye contact with Lopez, a small favor. It also muffles the cacophony of sounds from up above, the shouts of fighting men, the screams of falling men, the heavy weapons fire, the claxons warning of imminent destruction. This is a small comfort, overwhelmed in toto by the sight of the crater floor, still a couple of hundred meters below, imminent death expressed as geography. But this moment of relative privacy gives Hennessy another memory-flash, of his one and only direct interaction with the boss, some months ago. It was a strange conversation. He had decided that he wanted one of his stolen art masterpieces moved from one side of his luxurious quarters to another, and ordered somebody sent up to take care of it. By luck of the draw it was Hennessy, who went with trepidation, aware that the man had a reputation for feeding people to piranha for minor offenses. However, it happened to be a fairly civil occasion, during which the man actually looked at him like a person and made small talk about things like family, country, and political philosophy. Afterward, he offered Hennessy a glass of fine wine from his extensive collection, easily overriding the automatic refusal, and taking him to the glassed-in balcony where they both stood for a while, watching the many many levels of activity ranging from the domed ceiling to the cavern floor far below.

Hennessy had not known what the boss expected, whether this was a trap or an experiment in human resources, whether he was supposed to compliment the boss's grand vision or what. And then the boss said, "Do you know how one rises from almost nothing to create an enterprise on this scale?" Hennessy had understood then that he was here to provide an audience, and he said no, sorry, boss, I have absolutely no idea. And the boss said, "It is more than just vision, young man. Any number of people have vision. They build castles in the air, entire empires of wealth and accomplishment, dreams within dreams, ephemeral as the blinking of an eye. That is because they retreat before it becomes real. Rather than send their bodies after their imaginations, they pull out, and are back in whatever predicament they were before. What they should do instead is invest all they are, and dive in, as I did." Hennessy had expressed a wholly natural lack of comprehension and the boss had said, "Can you not see? What you are looking at right now is the living dream of the boy I was at fifteen, confined to a cot in a refugee camp; and I assure you that boy still exists, somewhere, still in that filthy place, still hungry and still hating the world enough to plot his grand revenge; he is what fuels this. You and I and the world I will ravage are merely living it." Hennessy muttered a few words to indicate that he understood, though he really didn't, and the boss had nodded in apparent approval of his lack of imagination and dismissed him to return to his other daily tasks.

———

So now here he is, in the prime of his life but still dying, those rocks racing up at him faster than he ever would have believed, and the first stirrings of fear clutch at him, because he doesn't want to die. He is not foolish enough to believe that he doesn't deserve to die; no, not at all. He is, after all, a functionary of a vast genocidal paramilitary organization, willing to obey its orders even though those orders are corrupt and murderous. That cannot be denied, though it happens to also be true of anybody who ever put on the uniform of any nation, even those putatively fighting on the side of right. Honestly, if you ever say, "Yes, sir," to someone wearing military insignia, you are however well meaning giving your de facto consent to any number of innocents perishing in crossfire. Just as guys in silos in Nebraska don't live their lives suffering conniptions over the knowledge that they might be ordered to someday blow up the entire world, Hennessy never gave more than five minutes of thought to the awareness that he's helping to guard a facility that intends to someday loose a doomsday gas. So there's that. But it's more than that. He has, he confesses to himself, had to do any number of evil things. He's occasionally been sent on missions that involved vast amounts of gunfire on city streets, and was just a few days ago involved in a speedboat chase on the canals of Venice that involved entire fusillades of gunfire aimed at this very son of a bitch who just a few seconds ago threw him off the catwalk; and that was frankly irresponsible, because even though none of those rounds hit their intended target there were so many of them that some must have penetrated the surrounding buildings and wounded if not killed any number of civilians whose safety had not been taken into account. That was, he confesses to himself, a shitty thing to do.

———

Hennessy could come up with many other sins, committed on behalf of this employer or another, but of every foul thing he's ever done, the very worst was threatening the girl. He knows her name but even now can only think of her as The Girl, as that somehow makes what he did shittier. The thing is that the boss had recently kidnapped a professor whose knowledge was key to the fabrication of the Doomsday Gas, and the guy wouldn't impart his expertise at all until the boss threatened his daughter, promising all sorts of unspecified tortures if the guy didn't start making with the test tubes and whatnot right away. At the boss's behest

94

Hennessy had brandished a nasty, serrated knife and grinned sadistically while the boss said, "This is Gunter. He loves making pretty girls into ugly ones." Hennessy's first name was not Gunter, of course; it was Fred. Gunter just sounded more threatening, that's all. Nor did Hennessy enjoy making pretty girls into ugly ones; he was a minion, not a sick fuck. But it was his duty to persuade, and so his leered impressively, displaying the prosthetic gold tooth he had placed over an incisor, just to get into character. De Niro he wasn't. He wasn't even Hasselhoff. But that gold tooth and the little snort of amusement hinted at infinite derangement, a life spent making legions of pretty ones into ugly ones, an expertise even, and while she shrieked and writhed and her father cried, "You animals, don't hurt her, I'll do anything!", Hennessy had even felt the ghost of the satisfaction that so many grand thespians must luxuriate in, when the house lights come up and everyone in the audience rises to provide their thunderous applause. Later, of course, lying beside his own Theresa and feeling her heart beat next to his, he considered just how terrible he would have felt if some bastard working for some greater bastard had subjected her to such terror, even for a moment; how deeply he would burn for revenge if in the months or years to come she woke from nightmares or exhibited symptoms of post-traumatic stress disorder. He wishes he could go back in time and whisper in The Girl's ear, *Don't worry, it's just a put-on, he's only pretending*. And yet he cannot, because he knows one thing as well as he knows his own name, Fred not Gunther: that if the boss had given the order to go ahead, and he had refused, then the same ruination would have taken place at the hands of the next leering sociopath behind him. That was part of what it meant to be part of a machine. You are replaceable. The things even you won't do will be done without hesitation by others. And if it had occurred to you for more than five minutes that this was evil and that it should not be permitted to continue, it would have been you, setting those explosives and flipping your fellow minions off catwalks. You didn't because you were putting in your time and looking forward to moving on, with Theresa and the kid. That's human. But it also, Hennessy had to admit to himself now, makes him part of the problem. Honestly. He finds himself hoping The Girl gets rescued. It doesn't matter to him, now, and it would be one less hash mark on his conscience, for the couple of seconds he still has left to possess one. Damn it all.

———

A nd now that Hennessy is almost upon the rocks that will break him open and receive the blood that will soon be shared with the similar stains that are still Lopez and Wu, he thinks back to what the boss told him that day in his luxurious quarters, about visualization. He is at the end of his earthly existence and he does not wish to see death rush at him, so he closes his eyes and pours all he has into the creation of the future he prefers.

He is with his uncomprehending father, the drunken brute, saying, "I made many of your mistakes, but look at me; I am still a good man to my family, a guy who does right by them, who does not allow himself to repeat any your mistakes." He wants his father to admit that he was wrong, that he could have been a better man himself, but instead the piece of crap shakes his head and says, *But look at you, falling to your death because of the evil you've done, you're exactly who I was and exactly who you set out to be, I take satisfaction in you failing exactly the same way.* "No," Hennessy says, "I was good to my family," and the old bastard says, *You think so, but she lives in company housing, and if she even survives the mountain blowing up she will remember you as the piece of crap who put her and the child in danger, in a place that always scared her, that she could not escape for fear of being hunted down as a security risk.* "But she was happy with me." *She clung to you,* the old man says, *and that's not even remotely the same thing. She's like a Mafia wife, stupid. She's trapped within a cage that allows no interaction with the everyday world and though she does love you she wishes that all of you were living out in open air, somewhere else. Right now she's listening to the claxons and she knows that she's going to die and that the baby is going to die. She may be wrong, because an escape is always possible, but don't think you've done right by her. You have not. I am not going to give you the satisfaction of allowing approval from me to be your dying fantasy. It ain't gonna happen. Just ask her.*

And so he does, and in his fantasy she is as lusciously beautiful as only a beautiful woman can be when she wants to underline everything that makes her a creature of fantasy, hair gleaming, makeup perfect, curves to die for, but as much as he amends and revises and cannot remove that which he now realizes was always in her eyes, a furtiveness, a desperation, the look of a creature in a cage. *What do you want?* she says. *You want me to fall into bed and arch my back and perform for you, the way I do every night? Why not? I love you. You know I do. But since you signed up with these bastards I've also hated you a little. I'm not surprised at all that you've gotten us all killed. It was always in the cards. It was always coming, and I don't forgive you for that. Even if*

I live I won't forgive you for that, because even if I get out with or without our child the world will always see me as a person of interest with connections to a terrorist organization, and I'll never be able to find a haven so remote that just walking around will not get me recognized, tossed in a cell, and tortured forever for whatever intel I might have. You've damned me, Fred. Fuck you.

————

"I'll make it up to you," Hennessy's fantasy-self says, and a new scenario forms, one almost identical to his current situation as it takes place within this very same installation. In this scenario he is the one who set the explosives and is detected just as he's making his escape. He is racing along the catwalk dodging fire from up above when Lopez comes charging him, saying things like, "Have you gone crazy?" and "What are you doing?" Lopez slashes with his knife. Hennessy blocks it, grabs his one-time friend with by the wrist and the belt and flips him over the railing toward certain death on the rocks below. Lopez's scream dopplers as he plummets out of sight, and then it's Wu, Wu, who always beat him in the hand-to-hand combat training, but Hennessy is driven by justice now and will not be denied. A blow to throat and another when he is off balance and now Wu is falling, with an identical Wilhelm Scream as he too sinks from sight. So it goes, one after another, some falling to the left and some falling to the right, a few fortuitously sucking up the bullets from up above as Hennessy reaches the end of the catwalk and scrambles up the scaffolding to the higher level where he moved the art treasure for the boss, that one time, and even in this dying fantasy he understands what satisfaction the interloper gets out of this line of work, the sense of overwhelming power that comes from fighting to save the day, even it involves in killing a whole lot of people. Sorry, Dieter. *Pow!* Sorry, Murdoch. *Bang!* Sorry, Hans, Karl, Theo, Eddie, Franco, Uli, Fritz, Kristof, James, Alexander, Marco: *Kick, Stab, Slash, Throttle, Immolate, Blow Up, Otherwise Murder,* not a single one of you is slowing me down on my way to the boss, and here I go leaping past the flame throwers and over the trap door to the alligator pit and I find myself facing the boss, rising from his leather chair with an utter lack of concern in the good eye unaffected to the dueling scar, and, Hennessy notices now for the very first time, looking goddamned stupid in that Nehru jacket. "I should have known it would be you," the boss says. "Of all my associates, you always struck me as the one who walks alongside the gods of Death."

Hennessy knows now that he has done what the boss claims to have done, concocted this entire world out of his whole imagination, a place to inhabit just because it aggrandized himself. He fully believes now that the only thing that keeps him from living in it forever is defeating the megalomaniacal son of a bitch before him, and so he knows that he cannot allow the confrontation to come to diluted by even a moment of doubt. "I've been waiting for this," he says, stepping forward, not frightened at all. This time he has right on his side. This time he is fighting for everything he loves. This time he is fighting for oh god he doesn't even know what he's fighting for, not now, but the blood is pounding in his ears and one of the bombs he set chooses that moment to go off, shaking his entire body to the core.

He thinks, I never even saw Paris.

SHOCKING TALES
DON WEBB

I think it is great fun at times to bring back some of the great writers of the early incarnation of this magazine. As with Nina Kiriki Hoffman, Scott Edelman, Adam-Troy Castro, O'Neil De Noux, Rob Vagle, and Kristine Kathryn Rusch, Don Webb was in the original issues.

He has been writing and in the field of science fiction and fantasy and horror and mystery for as long as Kris and I have been. In other words, a very long time.

I used to go to a lot of science fiction, fantasy, and horror conventions and when Don started this wonderful story after one, I was flat hooked. Enjoy.

SHOCKING TALES

DON WEBB

Tony Ray thought the whole thing up after World Horror Con was in Austin, TX. About a week after. It began as a group email about a dozen of us.

"Hey, I liked meeting you at the con! Let's get together to eat or watch movies or something."

There were writers, booksellers, artists, a guy that dressed up like a vampire, and some musicians that played spooky rock covers. About ten folks answered, and we batted ideas around. One guy owned, or I think his uncle owned, a share in a BBQ place near downtown. He said we could rent the upstairs room on Thursday nights for next to nothing—if we always cleared out by ten, tipped well, and bought family style.

Well, that got rid of the vegans.

Third Thursdays it was.

At first we would read our new work, or some neglected story that we thought was worthwhile. The vampire guy knew lots of scary history of Austin. He did a ghost tour and a murder tour. We finally decided on the Rule. We also came up with our clever name, the Shocking Tales Society.

On a rotating basis each member had to provide the entertainment. It could be a ghost story or a true crime story or anything else that was shocking. The group dropped from nine to seven. So, we tipped a little more. We always ordered drinks before and after the meal. And we chugged on for five years and then Lisa moved to London. Six seemed a little small so we decided to expand. Our first new member was Eric, who was a screenwriter and had two good, one okay and one sorry movie to his credit. Some of us words-in-row guys and gals were a little dubious, but that guy could sling a yarn.

Then came Katie.

It was the November meeting and many of us were kissing up to the management by buying deep-fried turkeys or smoked turkeys for next week. She walked at 7:05. Five minutes late and she was stunning. She wore a low-cut black dress. Her age was in the twenties and her bust size was in the upper thirties, if you get my drift. As a group I think our average age was fifty-five. Five guys, one gal (before Katie). Four white, one Hispanic, and one guy from the Indian subcontinent. Middle class—but certainly at both ends of that broad distinction. She made excuses. Traffic. I suspect her low-cut dress made enough excuses for most of us. She was better dressed than any of us, except maybe Huzaifa, who wore his impeccable gray suit. I was in jeans and a polo shirt that needed washing. Even before it got so much blood on it. She sat across from Tony and me.

Katie ordered a dark and stormy, then asked Tony to drink it. She hated to drink and drive she said but was aware of the customs of our "Ancient and Respectable Brotherhood." Then she looked at Joan and added, "And Sisterhood." And we all laughed.

We passed around the brisket and the links and the chicken. We passed the coleslaw and the potato salad. Some of us had warm peach cobbler and Bluebell vanilla ice cream. Katie and Joan had the New York cheesecake. After dinner there were drinks, and Katie handed me her Black Russian, which is my favorite cocktail. Then it was story time. Outside was dark but we could see the constant traffic on the road below. The waiter came in and cleared. He knew the drill.

Katie was almost too quiet to hear at first, but as she spoke she gained confidence. Her language and accent were cultured at first, but as she grew into her topic slang and F-bombs appeared. She put her small purse on the table where her plate had been. Every now and again she stroked it as though it were a pet. The waiter brought her hot tea, cream, and sugar as she began to speak.

"My name is Katie Bergson. I am humbled to be among you. I've been a horror fan all my life. Growing up I was a sickly child in New Orleans and my grandfather's library was a great comfort with its Arkham House first editions. Of course, *Twilight Zone, Night Gallery,* and *Tales from the Crypt* were my special delights and growing blocks from where Anne Rice lived made certain that vampires caught my eye. When I was eighteen a tragedy struck. A drunk driver took out my grandfather and my mom. Having been homeschooled by the former and over-sheltered by the latter I was grossly unprepared for the world. But I had help from my guardian. But more on that later. I should assure you that this isn't the Be Sorry for Katie Bergson hour. Tonight's theme is murder."

We were all hooked except for Tony. He gave a strong

glance at Huzaifa. I figured it was a client-attorney glance. In other words, I thought I wouldn't ever know its import. Katie seemed unfazed.

"My guardian was also my attorney. Or more properly my grandfather's attorney. He gave me the bare facts. If I liquidated my home, and grandad's collections, and added that money to my trust I would be fine. Not Rockefeller fine, not Donald Trump fine, but schoolteacher fine—with occasional splurges fine. It was hard to leave New Orleans. I loved the city, but I had no peers there. I didn't know anybody my age, and it would kill my soul to see granddad's mansion while I lived in an apartment. So, I went to Doublesign, Texas—not too far south from here. It's close enough that I can drive into Austin for events and far enough away that my money goes further. It wasn't a wholly random choice; I had a first cousin that lived there. She was the second person I murdered."

It was the habit of the Shocking Tales Society to leave our little room unlit during the tales and by now it was dark enough for me not to see my friends' reactions, but I thought Katie was doing fine.

"I've met enough writers and artists to know what's going through your minds now. Wow, if I had *that* setup I could make art full time. That would be paradise. But I didn't have that urge at all. I've never looked at a magazine and thought 'I'd like to write for them.' Or visited a gallery and thought, 'I can do that!' I'm just not wired that way. My health was good, except for some little pink pills I take for blood pressure, I'm sturdy, I don't need to live near a medical complex. So, I lived in Doublesign and bought scary books and rented scary movies and even came to Austin for scary plays. Occasionally I'd go on a hike with my cousin, who thought all my scary interests at best macabre and at worst a sign of mental illness. At first I found myself growing rather plump—after all, my main occupations were eating, sleeping, and consuming scary media. But I didn't care for seeing so much of me in the mirror. My cousin applauded. 'You are looking good now. You can find yourself a man!'"

She took a long sip of her tea.

"But I found I didn't want a man. Or for that matter a woman either. Not that I mentioned *that* option to my cousin; she and her husband, Eliot, were world class homophobes. My cousin bugged me to see her therapist who told me I had grief issues. She also told me to find some way to spend my time like volunteering at the church or reading to retarded children. She warned me of boredom and gave me an open prescription for Xanax. Church was dull—it was based on a sense of guilt I was profoundly missing. Retarded children were retarded. But he was right about one thing: I did grow bored. Doublesign isn't exactly the excitement capital of Texas. Heck, it's not even the most exciting town in its county."

Joan sniggered. I remembered she had "people" in Doublesign.

"At first I simply went the route of more extreme. There are extreme writers, extreme films, Internet nasties. One of you is even responsible for one of them." She grinned and we looked at Eric in the dark. "But films and horror comics and so forth have a flatness. Not yours, of course. But you can only flog the imagination so many times. I thought about what to do. Buy art, yes, Mr. Bendel—you do recognize me from the Dealer's Room." Another grin. "I even thought of getting your 'Yidhra's Cauldron' tattooed on my back. I tried not taking my Xanax. I tried buying weed from high schoolers at Sam

Houston High School. Once I even tried driving drunk. But I was empty. My cousin thought I needed Jesus. But one night it came to me. It was a full moon, a lovely Beaver Moon, as the *Farmer's Almanac* labels November's full moon. Venus was bright. The air was crisp. And the answer was murder. I left my two-room apartment on Old Dallas Road, and I walked to Memorial Park, and there among the names of Doublesign's World War Two dead I thought about murder. For weeks I was drunk on the idea. I even bought a handgun. Then I thought, 'You are being crazy bitch.' Prison is apt to be more boring than Texas. So, I gave my handgun to Eliot, who was sort of a gun nut.

"One afternoon my landlady, Doris Reyes, had an emergency. The good people of my apartment building were at work being teachers, and guys at the oil change place and short order cooks—but I was home. A wasp stung Doris as she cleaned our little pool, and she began swelling up something awful and having trouble breathing and knocked on my door. She could barely speak. Could I take her to the hospital? Well of course. I told her to take some Benadryl for the histamine, while I got dressed. I remembered my bottle as nearly empty. 'You can take all the ones from my medicine chest! Don't worry about too much.'

"I got dressed and she was quiet but breathing better. I drove her to the Doublesign Urgent Care clinic, our version of a hospital. We walked in. I signaled the nurses and they rushed toward Doris. Doris responded by dropping to the floor. She died even before they got her to a back room. Poor Doris. Anaphylaxis, they said.

"I drove home, pretty flustered. In my bathroom Doris hadn't found the Benadryl bottle with its two and a half pills.

She had emptied my blood pressure medicine with its five pills. Not a crazy mistake. I had them in a clear bottle. I hated the childproof bottle they came in. She had opened my medicine chest instead of the drawer. I had never thought of how much the small oval pink pills look like Benadryl. Of course, taking five was a crazy idea but Doris wasn't exactly the sharpest pencil in the box. I was blameless. I mean, I hadn't meant to kill her.

"Or had I? I'd always found her annoying with her loud *ranchera* music and her badly thought-out politics and her 'No pool after nine' rule. Maybe my subconscious did the deed. I worried that there would be an inquest or an autopsy. Instead, her son invited me to the funeral and the priest said that I had been trying to save her life. And the family gave me *three* months of free rent.

"Then I realized that I'm a soft-spoken good-looking woman and I could kill as many people as I want. I've killed thirty-two so far and by the end of tonight, I'll bring it to thirty-three, my grandfather's favorite number. He was a Freemason. Thirty-third degree; I think that's the top. The El Supremo.

"Now I couldn't use my gun or probably poison again. I would use my brain. I suddenly found I was creative. I was an Artist. My next few weeks were blissful, but soon boredom came my way. One Tuesday evening as a lovely thunderstorm was brewing I was chatting with my cousin. I wanted to shock her, and I started to tell her about Doris, but drew back and confessed to having bought a rather expensive dual-headed vibrator. She gave her Foursquare Gospel gasp, and then to my surprise had a 'confession' to tell me. 'When my son died of lung cancer, Eliot and I resolved to give up smoking. I failed. I still smoke three or four cigarettes a day and I spend half my brain hiding this from him. Only you and my prayer partner, Mary Anne, know.'

"'Is Mary Anne some old church biddy?' I asked. 'Oh no,' laughed Suzy. 'She is a young single woman, sort of a prettier version of me.' I realized that lovely Fate had just sent me a victim. 'I helped Grandpa quit smoking—not that it did him much good—and I can help you. If you follow my instructions.'

"'Anything,' she said.

"Grandpa paid for this cure. He gave a hundred dollars to a *gris-gris* woman who told the cards in Jackson Square. First buy a journal. Leave the first page blank and then chronicle your efforts. Then I will give you a coffee can. A souvenir from Louisiana. Everyday throw your butts in it. When it's full, you will drive to a cemetery and bury it. Then come home and write in the first page of your journal your victory! Now to keep the journal safe from Eliot's eyes, leave it at my apart-ment.' She nodded with the big-eyed look Southern Protes-tants give to hoodoo. I rummaged around and found a slightly rusty old Community Coffee can. The dark roast with chicory that our granddad loved. I emptied the pens and pencils and scissors it held. 'Take this. Hide it in your garage.' Every day I studied her handwriting, practicing it until I could do it perfectly as I read of her weak-willed attempts to give up smoking. She even thoughtfully chronicled where she had hidden the can. A few weeks passed and I went to their home while they labored like good middle-class Americans. I was armed with a small trash bag and an old-fashioned can opener. Suzy had stashed the butt can in the darkest corner of their two-car garage atop an old trunk. I emptied its contents into my trash bag, then I used the can opener to open the other end of the coffee can, making it a cylinder. I moved the trunk and placed a large gas can under the open cylinder. Suzy got home every day at five-oh-five (as she dutifully journaled) and then ran to the garage for a quick smoke, giving her enough time to brush her teeth before Eliot rolled in at five thirty. Of course today she would toss her butt in the dark into a half empty five gallon can and...

"*Boom!*"

Some of us jumped. Katie continued, "And so it was! Everyone was perplexed by Suzy's death. Why had she been in the garage? How had the gas ignited? Eliot blamed himself for keeping so much gas. It was a lovely funeral. Eliot was distraught for weeks. One day he dropped by and was telling me that all he had had in life were Suzy and their cancer-slain son, Brandon. He admitted to suicidal thoughts and was seeing Doublesign's only psychologist, Dr. Fatima Ortiz. 'Oh, poor Eliot.' I said, 'Did you know Suzi kept a diary? She had me keep it here but made me promise to never look at it. I think you should have it.' 'You haven't read it?' he asked. 'Of course not! You know how close she and I were.'

"I gave him the diary. I had created a beginning. She blamed Eliot for Brandon's death, saying he hadn't prayed hard enough, and revealed that Suzy was now sleeping with her attractive prayer partner, Mary Anne. But Mary Anne had rejected her for her smoking. Then there were fourteen entries in her own hand chronicling her attempts to stop smoking. Then a last entry telling of a terrible fight with Mary Anne, who rejected her because of her tobacco-tasting coochie, and her plan to blow herself up in the garage.

"Poor Eliot. He couldn't deal with the guilt, so he shot

himself. I had hoped for a murder-suicide involving Mary Anne, but we don't always get what we want. Neither Eliot nor Suzy had mentioned me in their will, but Eliot's father let me take what I wanted. Suzi's 'diary' and one of Eliot's many handguns. Of course it was my old gun."

At this point Katie looked at her purse again. Her sense of drama was excellent.

"Of course, I don't have time to tell you about all of my murders, but I have made a list."

She opened her purse and took out a small battery powered "candle" that she switched on. It was a cheap Christmas decoration—it looked like a dripping wax candle with a tiny wreath around its base. She then took out a cream-colored envelope, which she lay on the table. She took a long sip of tea. I could see a metal cylinder—maybe a gun barrel— in her opened bag. She winked at me and continued.

"Most of the killings were planned out in detail, which was (of course) part of the fun. But a couple were spontaneous as fuck. One day I was standing in the parking lot of my apart- ment when a guy drove up in a Mercedes with New York plates honking his horn at me. 'Can you help me? My dad is having a heart attack and his doctor is Dr. Ortiz? Can you tell me where his office is?' I knew he meant Dr. Roland Ortiz, the cardiologist, not his daughter Dr. Fatima Ortiz. Time was clearly of the essence. He was only a block from his dad's doctor's office. I explained how to get to Dr. Fatima Ortiz's office, which was about a mile out of town between Double- sign and Flapjack. 'Be rally loud when you get there, he may be slow to open up.' 'Thank you a million!' He sped off. According to the weekly newspaper his poor dad died in Dr. Ortiz's parking lot. The sheriff questioned me. I said the man

had asked for directions to Dr. Ortiz's office but had said
nothing about his father or a heart attack. He seemed so upset
that I thought he wanted a shrink. I acted overcome by guilt. I
saw Dr. Ortiz again for about a month this time. I think she
really helped me.

"Well, I could go on for hours, but I've heard that you
gentlemen, excuse me—you gentlemen and lady—like your
tales to be short and end in high drama. It took me a long time
to decide whether Doris could be counted as a murder. It was
(at least consciously) an accident. But since I took so much glee
in it, I decided that was murder number one. I did number
thirty-two last night here in Austin. I drove in near midnight. I
wanted to shop at the Arboretum this morning and of course
to attend this noble assemblage tonight. Of course, the road to
Doublesign goes to Pennypacker Bridge. There was a young
woman of color standing on the wrong side of the railing over
the lake. Who knows what horrors had led her to contem-
plating self-destruction? I parked my little white Honda at the
end of the bridge and walked quietly up to her. I watched a
series of emotions pass over her brown face illuminated by the
mercury vapor lamps on the bridge. Fear, anger, confusion,
and finally a brief smile. She had come to a happy ending and
was about to climb back over the railing. With all my might I
yelled, 'Don't do it!' I must have startled the poor dear. She
twitched in confusion and fell into the water. Of course, I ran
to my phone and called nine-one-one saying I had seen the
poor girl plunge. Based on the article in today's *Statesman*, I
guess she didn't have a chance. The physics of inertia being
what they are, internal organs tend to keep going. The force of
impact causes them to tear loose. Autopsy reports typically
indicate that the jumpers have lacerated aortas, livers, spleens,

and hearts. Ribs are often broken, and the impact shoves them into the heart or lungs."

Tony Ray interrupted the narrative.

"That's fucking grotesque. There was a suicide on the Pennypacker Bridge last night. We don't make fun of real human loss here. That's why we put up with stuff like Don's lame Lovecraft pastiches. I am going to ask you to leave."

I felt pretty called out by that. Why single me out as the bad storyteller? I mean, Joan's stuff is pretty lame.

Katie calmly opened her bag and drew forth the handgun. "All I claimed to do is give you a shocking story. I told you (and your lawyer Mr. Huzaifa) that it would be the most shocking tale this little group of minor thrill-seekers ever heard. How fucking dare you criticize me?"

She pointed the gun at Tony Ray's chest and pulled the trigger. It was shockingly loud.

Our ears were still ringing but we could hear Katie's and Tony's laughter.

Tony was ecstatic. "The look on your faces! That was the best!"

Katie said, "It's a prop gun. When I asked Mr. Ray to join we agreed on all of it. Even telling the staff below not to run up. Was my story memorable? Go ahead, shoot me with it."

She handed me the gun. I was surprised at its weight, but I hadn't handled guns since my daddy's .38 forty years ago. Still stinging from Tony's remark, I fired across the table. Her chest blossomed with red jelly. I dropped the gun because of its kick. I kept expecting her or Tony to laugh. Of course, it wasn't a prop gun, just a gun that had been loaded with a blank, then live ammunition. The staff ran up and turned on all the lights. It felt like two in the morning, when lights banish barflies and bring a shock of leaving the womb. I was crying and Tony (almost as blood-spattered as me) began talking rapidly with Huzaifa. As we waited for the police, Joan opened the envelope. From the cream-colored paper she read a list of thirty-three names from Doris Reyes to Katie Bergson.

MISSING CAROLYN

ANNIE REED

Professional writer Annie Reed writes stories that span genres and are always powerful. In fact with Annie, you just never know the type of story you might be reading, but you will always know it will grab you and be a compelling read.

So far Annie has had a story in every issue of Pulphouse Fiction Magazine *and as the editor, I hope to continue that streak. You will understand why after you read this gripping story.*

Her stories have appeared in four best mystery stories of the year volumes so far. Look for so much more of this prolific writer's work at her website https://anniereed.wordpress.com/

MISSING CAROLYN

ANNIE REED

T he house felt too big.

Alex still expected Carolyn to be there when he got home from work. His job took him into the city, an hour commute each way if the traffic cooperated, two if it didn't. She always beat him home even if she had to make a last-minute run to the bank or the post office. The difference between working for a high-powered law firm in the financial district and a dental office in the suburbs.

He'd installed a motion sensor light over the front door and another inside the entryway. Too little, too late, but at least the house wasn't dark when he keyed open the front door and stepped inside.

Cold and big and empty, yes, but not dark.

He should get a dog, someone at the office had said. Something to keep him company.

He'd heard the remark in passing. Watercooler gossip in the breakroom from people who probably didn't know he was standing just beyond the door trying like hell to remember

121

where he'd been going and what he was supposed to be doing.

The remark had stuck with him.

Get a dog. As if a dog could replace the woman he'd loved since he'd been a junior in high school. The woman he'd expected to grow old with. To travel the world with once they both retired. Wasn't that the American dream? Work hard, live responsibly, and put away enough money to enjoy your golden years with the one person you couldn't live without?

Welcome to the American nightmare.

Alex put his briefcase down on the tiled floor of his entryway next to the coatrack. The motion sensor's blue-white light made the gray tiles and the off-white walls in the entry look ghostly cold and uninviting.

Except for the faint creaks of the house settling in the chill of the night, the only sounds were his own breathing and the scrape of his shoes on the slate tiles. The house was still full of their furniture, but the motion sensor light didn't reach that far into the darkness. Except for the entryway table, he might as well have been standing in some stranger's abandoned home. A place someone had slapped a fresh coat of paint on and put back on the market in the hope of finally catching a good sale.

The house even smelled stale.

No enticing aromas coming from the kitchen with a promise of a comfortable evening filled with good food, fine wine, and sitting on the couch together in front of the fire after a long, hard day at work.

They'd never had kids—both of them were too busy—and except for every other Friday night when Carolyn came to the city after she got off work so they could treat themselves to a well-deserved night on the town, they spent most evenings cuddled up beneath a fleece throw Carolyn had bought at one of the stores in the mall all the Goth kids went to. Sometimes they made it to the bedroom, but sometimes they didn't. Carolyn called the nights they made love on the couch their "romance movie" nights.

He loved their romance movie nights.

She'd laughed when she'd told him how the pierced and wildly tattooed clerk had tried not to look shocked when the frumpy, middle-aged woman had shown up at the register to buy a fleece for one of the metal bands featured on the store's sound system.

Frumpy had been Carolyn's word for herself. To Alex, she had always been the beautiful woman he'd stood next to in front of all their friends and pledged to love and protect for the rest of their lives.

The fleece had caught her eye as she walked past the store in the mall. She'd bought it because she liked the art. She thought it was pretty.

The artwork featured a skeleton crawling out of a grave.

That was Carolyn, finding beauty in everything.

He'd thrown the fleece away. The company he'd hired to clean up the house had gotten the blood out, but he'd still smelled it. Saw clots of it on the skeleton's grinning face along with bits of things he didn't want to think about.

He flipped on the light switch next to the front door, and lights came on over the stairs in the upstairs hallway. Warm light instead of the motion sensor's ghostly blue-white light.

He clicked the motion sensors off with a remote and trudged up the steps, loosening his tie. He grabbed a beer from the small refrigerator in the upstairs utility room and took a long drink. He didn't turn on the flat screen television or the stereo in the bedroom, an expensive entertainment package they'd bought each other as a tenth wedding anniversary gift.

That had been fifteen years ago. They'd never thought about replacing any of the components. The things still worked, and they'd been saving up for retirement. The only things they'd really splurged on were the two Friday nights out every month and Carolyn's laptop. She bought herself a new one every year.

He could throw the whole thing out the window now and it wouldn't matter anymore. Carolyn had always been the music lover. The one who liked to watch movies before bed. He used to think he preferred silence, but he'd never really known what silence was until after Carolyn was gone.

The first night he'd come back to his empty, quiet house after the police had released the crime scene.

After he'd paid someone to clean away Carolyn's blood.

That had been silence. Total and absolute and unrelenting.

Alex showered like he did every night, then he put on black jeans and a black turtleneck. He took another beer from the fridge and a gun from the lockbox beneath the bed, then he went to sit in the dark on the landing halfway down the stairs to the first floor.

He sat in the dark in his quiet house like he did every night, beer in his left hand, gun in his right.

Waiting for the bastards to come back.

Home invasion, the police told him.

Burglary gone bad.

"Probably been watching your house for a while," the police said. "Knew your routine better than you did. Just didn't expect your wife to be home."

Carolyn had taken a rare sick day. The flu had been going around, and some parent had brought their sick kid in for dental work rather than reschedule. Kids were little germ factories. No matter how careful the dental assistants were with their own hygiene, someone inevitably got sick, and then the whole office got sick.

That Friday it had been Carolyn's turn. She'd even joked about it.

"Bring me home some Dairy Queen," was the last thing she would ever say to him.

She'd had a soft spot for soft serve.

Except he'd worked too late that Friday night to pick up Dairy Queen on his way home. His call to let Carolyn know he wouldn't be home until midnight had gone straight to her voicemail.

The police wouldn't tell him if she'd already been dead when he called. Maybe they wanted to spare his feelings.

Or maybe they just didn't know.

She always parked her car in the garage. Alex parked his in the driveway. After Alex left for work, the place had looked deserted.

She must have fallen asleep on the couch beneath the fleece. Forgotten to turn on any lights in the house.

He wondered when she'd first heard them. When they broke the little window next to the front door to flip the latch on the deadbolt? Or when they'd kicked in the panels on the front door after they'd discovered that the deadbolt was keyed on both sides?

The front door had been made of natural oak, but the decorative panels had been inserts. It didn't take a martial artist to kick holes in the front door by kicking out a panel or two.

Carolyn hadn't tried to call 9-1-1. The police had found her cell phone on the kitchen counter next to a cold cup of tea.

At least Alex hadn't been the one to find her. He'd lost count of how many people had said that to him. "At least you were spared that."

That particular honor had gone to a pair of teenagers who'd been walking the neighborhood trying to sell coupon books for a high school fundraiser. They'd noticed the broken front door and called the police.

But not before they'd looked inside.

They probably regretted that decision for a long time.

Carolyn had been sprawled on the living room floor just beyond the entryway, the fleece blanket wrapped around her upper body, her blood soaked into the carpet from where her head had been bashed in.

The living room had been ransacked. A lamp with a crystal base Carolyn had inherited from her mother had been smashed on the fireplace hearth. Books, including a few signed first editions, had been pulled off a built-in bookshelf, one of the features that had sold them on the house. Pages had been ripped out of the books, and the bindings torn. Artwork that Carolyn had picked out had been pulled down off the walls, the frames trashed, the prints shredded. Knickknacks that Carolyn had collected during her teenage years had been grabbed off the mantel over the fireplace and thrown against the wall, bits of porcelain stuck in the carpet.

Random destruction.

The only things stolen had been her wallet, her laptop, and a tablet.

And Carolyn's life.

"They took easy things to turn into cash," the police told him. "Probably high, looking for an easy score."

At least Alex and Carolyn didn't have any guns in the house. He'd heard that comment a lot, too.

No, they didn't have any guns. Not then.

The police had dusted a few flat surfaces for fingerprints. They took his for comparison, and he assumed they took Carolyn's. Later. But after a month, they'd made no arrests.

After six weeks, he figured they never would.

After seven, he bought a gun.

And came up with a plan.

———

The first thing he did was to buy a new laptop.

He didn't need it. He never brought work home— that had been Carolyn. He never even turned the new laptop on. He just took it out of the box and put the empty box on top of his garbage can nearly a week before the garbage was scheduled for pickup.

He bought motion sensor lights he could turn on and off with a remote. He turned the sensors off every night as soon as he made it through the door and made sure he was the only one in the house.

He started parking his own car in the garage. He covered

the broken window by the front door with cardboard and duct tape.

And he bought a gun.

He knew next to nothing about guns. He still didn't. He'd gone to a gun shop and bought one he could hold and load, point and shoot. A pistol, not a revolver.

Something that held more than six bullets.

Something that didn't need to be registered.

Was this a great country or what?

A few days later he bought a new game system. Top of the line. No games, just the system. He unpacked it and put it on the bed in the guest bedroom. He leaned the empty box alongside his garbage can next to the empty computer box.

He hated video games. He'd played a few when he was a kid, but he sucked at them. He could never get the combination of buttons down right. His characters jumped when they should have punched, ran into walls when they should have been running at the bad guys. He always chose the wrong weapon to use against the monsters. He certainly wasn't going to put in the time to learn a new game now.

But if you were going fishing, you needed bait.

————————

Alex had almost finished his beer when the doorbell rang.

He limited himself to two beers a night, the first to numb himself to the pain of coming home to the empty house he'd shared with Carolyn, the one true love of his life, and the second to give him the patience to wait.

But he hadn't put out bait to attract anyone who'd ring a doorbell.

Alex ignored it.

After a few moments, the doorbell rang again.

Then someone pounded on the door.

He'd replaced the broken oak door with another one almost exactly like it, complete with decorative panel inserts. Easy to bust out with the right kind of kick.

Easy to use as a weapon.

The bastards who'd broken into his house had used a kicked-out door panel to beat Carolyn to death. The police had found it next to her body, which had been wrapped in her fleece blanket with the artwork skeleton crawling out of a grave.

"Mr. Crawford, I know you're in there," came a voice from the other side of his locked front door. "Open up. Police."

The voice was female, the pounding on the door authoritative.

Alex stretched out his stiff legs and stood up. He walked down the dark stairs and turned on the motion sensor lights with the remote.

The dark-haired woman standing in the ghostly blue-white light on his front step wasn't dressed in a police uniform, but she had that compact air of authority he'd come to associate with the police ever since Carolyn's death.

"You have identification?" he asked anyway.

She showed him her badge—a gold detective's shield.

"Morrisey," she said, introducing herself. "May I come in?"

He backed away from the door, an unspoken invitation, and went to turn on a light in the living room.

"You always carry your gun in the house?" she asked as she closed the front door behind herself.

He'd forgotten he even still had it.

"Seemed like a wise idea," he said. "Given recent events." He lifted his nearly empty beer bottle. At least he still remembered he was carrying that. "Want a beer, or are you on duty?"

"No. And no."

He thought about getting himself another beer from the fridge in the kitchen and decided against it. Instead he plopped himself down on the couch where he and Carolyn used to snuggle in front of the fireplace and sometimes make love. The fireplace was gas, easy enough to light, but he didn't plan to ever turn it on again.

The cop—Morrisey—sat down in an easy chair off to one side of the couch and looked at him.

"You mind putting that down?" she asked him, nodding toward the gun.

He dropped the gun on the couch next to where he sat.

"You have anything to tell me?" he asked. "Anything about the case?"

He already knew the answer—nothing new; sorry, Mr. Crawford—but lawyers were trained that was how to cross-examine a hostile witness. Never ask a question if you didn't already know the answer.

Morrisey leaned forward in the chair. "Want to tell me what the hell you're doing?" she asked, ignoring his questions.

"Not having a beer with you."

The response came out fast—glib and sarcastic—but he couldn't seem to help himself. Sometime over the last few weeks he'd quit thinking that the police were good guys out there busting their butts trying to find his wife's killers.

"You're carrying a gun inside your own house," she said. "Sitting in the dark by yourself on a Friday night." She glanced around the room. "I don't see your new game system anywhere. You have it upstairs? With your new laptop?"

Trash had been picked up two days ago. The laptop and game console boxes were landfill by now.

"You been spying on me?" he asked.

"We've had units in the neighborhood. They pay attention. But I'm guessing that's not the kind of attention you're hoping to attract."

He didn't say anything. That was another thing they taught you in law school—how to keep your mouth shut.

She leaned forward in the easy chair, elbows on her knees. "You're playing a dangerous game. I think you're smart enough to know that."

He looked toward the dark, empty fireplace.

He wasn't smart. If he'd been smart, he would have come home from work on time so he could bring his sick wife her Dairy Queen. So he could have turned on the lights in the house so the robbers—the killers—would know someone was home and pass his house right on by.

The hell of it was that the deal he'd stayed late that night to hammer out had been revised five times since then.

His work had been a waste.

The whole damn, sad, sorry mess had been a waste. He'd cancelled Carolyn's credit cards while he'd still been in shock that night, and the killers never had a chance to use them. She didn't carry much cash in her wallet, maybe forty dollars tops. Her laptop was worth maybe five hundred bucks, her tablet a couple hundred more.

That's was what her life had been worth. Less than eight

hundred dollars. What he billed his clients for two hours' work.

"Are you going to find the people who killed my wife?" he asked the detective. "Give her justice?"

Give him peace?

Just one night of peace?

He wished he'd grabbed another beer before he sat down on the couch.

"We're doing our best," she said. "But you have to give us a chance. Don't go adding to the problem."

The problem.

This case hadn't been just a simple smash and grab. A woman had died. It was like no one remembered that.

He closed his eyes. The muscles of his jaw ached from holding back his temper.

"I'll keep that in mind," he said. "Will there be anything else?"

She didn't answer, and eventually he opened his eyes to look at her.

Her cop expression had softened. For the first time he noticed that her eyes were as dark as her hair.

"I feel for you, Mr. Crawford," she said. "You might not believe that, but I do. You might not think we're trying to find your wife's killers, but we are. Junkies, meth heads, tweakers —one thing they all have in common is that they're stupid. They mess up. All they care about is their next score and they don't care what they have to do to get that. Eventually they screw up, and we'll be there to catch them. I want you to be alive when we do."

She stared at him for a long moment, and he thought she was going to say something like *your wife would want you alive, too*, but she surprised him. She simply got up from the chair and let herself out the front door without another word.

She dropped a business card on the table by the front door before she left.

He didn't have the heart to go back to sitting on the landing in the dark. His heart ached in a way he wouldn't have thought possible only a few months ago.

He took out his cell phone to look at the time—not quite ten at night—but his eyes strayed to his voicemail icon. He thumbed it on. Pushed "play" on the last voicemail from his wife and put the phone to his ear.

He listened while she talked about a small frustration at work. Not really the reason for her call, she said. She wanted to let him know she'd be stopping by the store on her way home, did he want her to pick up anything special for dinner?

Her voice had been cheerful, the message nothing special. Just the type of message that married people left for each other. But now it was everything special. It was the only voice-mail message she'd left him that he hadn't deleted before she'd been killed. Now he wished that he'd saved every single one.

He closed his eyes as he listened to the message again. And again. And five more times before he finally made himself stop.

Before he went up to bed he got another beer from the kitchen refrigerator. The remnants of last night's takeout sat in sad little boxes on the top shelf of the fridge. He thought about eating leftover chow mein, then closed the refrigerator door and went upstairs to bed.

He never heard the burglars break into his house until they were already through his new front door.

———

He should have stopped at two beers.

Three beers on an empty stomach and an empty, shattered heart had been too much. He'd fallen into a deep, dreamless sleep. He didn't hear anything until the fourth stair from the top creaked under a stealthy footfall.

He'd told Carolyn he would fix the creak if she wanted, but she'd said that was her early warning system for those nights when he was working late.

"So I can give my man-on-the-side time to hide in the closet," she'd said.

An old joke between the two of them. Her "man on the side" and his "girl at the office." Their version of "the list"—celebrities they were each allowed to sleep with, as if the occasion would ever arise.

He'd been so in love with her the thought had never even occurred to him that he might find someone else attractive. Even now—especially now—he couldn't imagine sharing his life with anyone ever again.

The stair creaked, and he snapped awake.

Listened for the sound to come again as the intruder's foot lifted from the step.

After a moment, it did.

The hair on the back of his neck stood on end. He wasn't alone in the house.

He never once thought it was Carolyn, back from the grave like the skeleton on the fleece blanket he'd thrown away. He didn't believe in ghosts. He didn't believe in the walking dead or demons or monsters.

Except monsters of the human variety. The kind of

monsters who'd kill a sick woman in her own house just because she'd been in the way.

He reached for his gun. He always kept it on the bed next to him in the spot that had been Carolyn's. He still only slept on his side of the bed.

The gun wasn't there.

Of course, not. He'd left his gun on the couch. Forgotten it when he'd grabbed the third beer from the kitchen.

His head felt fuzzy, half stuffed with cotton, but his heart was beating double time.

He didn't have a weapon. He didn't have a way to fight back.

But he damn well sure wasn't going to be caught in his bed. Killed with a blanket wrapped around his head.

He slid from beneath the covers onto the bedroom floor and counted.

The squeaky riser was the fourth from the top.

The intruder would be careful now, waiting for another stair to creak. None of them did, but the intruder wouldn't know that. The police didn't think the robbers who'd killed Carolyn had made it upstairs. None of her jewelry had been taken. Alex had gambled on the assumption that the killers would come back to steal what they had missed.

The gamble had paid off, but he'd gone to bed unprepared.

He counted down from four slowly, imagining he was the killer on the stairs, placing each foot down easy, not sure if anyone was in the house. The cop—the detective—hadn't been here long. The killers could have missed her. Assumed that Alex no longer lived here since the house was always dark.

Alex scuttled across the bedroom floor, moving as quietly as he could, headed toward the entertainment center. Carolyn loved watching movies in bed, but their equipment had been old. Their Blu-ray player had been top of the line when they bought it, nearly the size of an old VCR with a heavy metal case. Carolyn had been talking about replacing it with a model that would let her stream some of the online services, but she hadn't done that yet.

He reached around the back of the Blu-ray player and pulled out all the wires, then lifted the heavy box up and held it two-handed over one shoulder like a baseball bat. He crept to one side of his bedroom door.

And then he waited.

His eyes were well adjusted to the dark. All those nights spent sitting in the dark on his stairs waiting for a moment just like this.

The burglar—the killer—took his time getting to the master bedroom. Alex heard the sound of wires rubbing on plastic, and then the rustle of cloth. The burglar must have gone into the guest bedroom first and found the unhooked game system. Probably slid it into a loot bag.

Easy money, boys. Go ahead and take the bait.

After a few more minutes, Alex finally saw movement at his bedroom door.

A gun—maybe his gun—followed by the hand and then the arm of the man sneaking into the master bedroom.

Alex made himself wait until the burglar—the killer—was through the doorway and Alex had a clear shot at the man's head.

He was a piss-poor excuse for a burglar (killer). He didn't even check the sides of the door.

Alex swung his wife's old Blu-ray player like a major league hitter aiming for the fences.

He hit the man square in the back of his head.

The impact sent numbing pain up Alex's arms all the way to his shoulders, and he nearly dropped the player.

The man dropped like a sack of cement on the bedroom carpet.

Alex hit him again. And again.

And again.

He was about ready to swing for the fifth time when he heard footsteps pounding up the stairs.

The burglar—the killer—wasn't alone.

Of course not. The police thought there'd been more than one killer in his house.

And if one of them were armed, both of them were armed. A dented Blu-ray player wasn't good enough against a killer who knew Alex was there.

He dropped the Blu-ray player and scrambled for the gun the burglar had dropped when Alex hit him.

His fingers closed around it the same time the other burglar (killer) burst through the bedroom door, gun arm extended in front of himself.

And tripped over the burglar Alex had brained with the Blu-ray player.

The burglar's shot went wide.

Alex fired the gun—his gun—over and over again until it clicked empty.

The second burglar dropped beside the first.

Neither man moved. Alex listened for any other sounds coming from downstairs, but his house was quiet again. Somewhere in the neighborhood a dog started barking.

They'd never had a dog. Never had any pets. Carolyn liked

animals a lot, and it broke her heart that she couldn't have any, but her allergies wouldn't allow it.

Alex crossed his bedroom floor to the nightstand, careful not to step in any blood. He took his cell phone off the charger and called the police.

"I want to report a break-in," he said.

He was on hold when the shakes hit, and for the first time since the night Carolyn died, he started to cry.

———————

This time Alex had to go to the station to give a statement. One of the other lawyers from the firm accompanied him just in case the questions got too intense, too pointed, but while the police didn't treat him gently, they treated him with respect.

The detective who took his statement wasn't Morrisey but a tired-looking, overweight man a few years short of retirement. He took Alex and his attorney into an interview room barely large enough for the three of them and the industrial gray desk and chairs. No art on the cinderblock walls, no one-way mirror, no discrete recording equipment. The detective used an app on his phone to record Alex's statement.

When the interview was over, the detective gave Alex a hard look.

"You're a lucky man," he said. "These two have been hitting houses all over the area. They're pros. Two-strike losers who've done hard time. They usually pick empty places filled with high-tech toys."

The detective paused, waiting for Alex to say something,

but Alex knew better. He was a lawyer. He could out-wait anybody.

"Guess they figured out you'd bought some new stuff," the detective eventually said.

Alex shrugged. It had been a long night, and it would be a long day. He had things he had to do. Replacing his front door wasn't one of them.

He hadn't heard the burglars break in the night before because they'd used a gadget to pick his lock. Apparently it was the same kind of tool law enforcement agencies used when they wanted to disable a lock without breaking down the door.

They hadn't kicked in his front door.

They hadn't been the same killers who beat Carolyn to death for the money in her purse and her laptop and her tablet.

The men who'd broken into his house the night before wouldn't be breaking into anyone else's house. Alex had killed the man he'd shot. The other man would be in the hospital for a long time, but he'd probably never know it. Alex had caved in the side of the man's skull with Carolyn's old Blu-ray player.

"Guess you're gonna need something new to play your movies," the detective said.

"I don't watch movies," Alex said. "That was my wife."

The detective knew about Carolyn. Her death and the prior break-in was part of the official statement.

"I'm real sorry about what happened to your wife," the detective said. "You probably weren't thinking straight when you bought your new stuff, but it's wise to break the boxes up and stuff them in the can. Better still if you do that the same day the trash is picked up. The bad guys tend to notice stuff like that. Guess you could say it's their job."

Alex closed his eyes as a wave of weariness passed over him.

He'd taken care of the men who'd broken into his house, but he hadn't taken care of the men who'd killed Carolyn. They were still out there. Still getting high and stealing what didn't belong to them and taking lives with no more thought than where their next fix was coming from.

"I'll be more careful," Alex said. "Guess I didn't think things through."

The detective stood up and shook Alex's hand. "We'll be in touch if we need anything."

Alex thanked the lawyer from his firm as they parted ways on the steps in front of the police station. The sun was just cresting the mountains to the east. Another brand-new day with only a hint of clouds overhead.

Carolyn used to love watching the sun rise. Sit at the kitchen table and have a cup of tea and read a chapter or two of a novel on her tablet. She didn't have to be at work until nine, but she got up every morning so that she could kiss Alex goodbye as he left for work. He only saw the sunrise in his rearview mirror as he navigated heavy traffic into the city.

Another wave of loss washed over him, this one so strong that it took his breath away. He had to actually concentrate on breathing.

Carolyn would never get to see another sunrise. Never hold him in her arms and give him a kiss and tell him to go get the bad guys.

She meant on behalf of his clients, but he could still hear

her words clear as day. Ever since her death, those words had taken on new meaning.

If he couldn't get the bad guys on behalf of his wife, what good was he?

He straightened his shoulders and scrubbed at his face. The lawyer from work had offered to give Alex a ride wherever he wanted to go—his house was a crime scene again—but Alex told the man he'd make his own way to the hotel he'd stayed at last time. He wanted time alone to think.

He had planning to do.

He had a new game system to buy. The other one he'd bought was now evidence.

So was his gun. He'd have to buy a new one.

Maybe more than one. He needed a gun he could leave upstairs all the time.

And another tablet. A high-end one that came in a big box. He'd have to research which one was considered the best.

Which model was the easiest to turn into quick cash.

He was still making plans when he heard someone call his name. A woman's voice.

He turned around to see Detective Morrisey coming down the stairs toward him.

"Detective," he said.

"I just read your statement," she said.

He kept his face carefully neutral. "I didn't know you were assigned to the case."

"They're related. I got copied." She gave him a hard look. "I get copied on anything that relates to you or to your wife's death."

He nodded. "That helps you catch who killed her?"

"We're working on it."

He hadn't expected anything different or he wouldn't have asked the question.

He started to turn away when she called his name again.

"You might want to consider a new hobby," she said. "This happens again, we might look at you a little harder. You're a lawyer. You know we can charge you."

He didn't say anything.

"Find something else to take up your time," she said. "Something you can care for besides yourself. Get a dog. They need a lot of attention. Help get you out of your head."

He allowed himself a small smile that he was sure didn't reach his eyes.

"Can't," he said. "My wife's allergic."

THE PURPLE SIDE OF BLUE

O'NEIL DE NOUX

O'Neil De Noux takes his amazing skills as one of the best writers of detective fiction working today and gives us another amazing story. O'Neil has published about fifty novels with more coming regularly. His awards include The United Kingdom Short Story Prize, the Shamus Award (for best private eye fiction), the Derringer Award (for excellence in mystery short fiction) and Police Book of the Year.

Two of his stories have appeared in the prestigious Best American Mystery Stories *annual anthology and I noticed he had another in the recommended reading for this year's volume. He won the Shamus for a story in 2020. You can find out a lot more about his work at his website http://www.oneildenoux.com/*

THE PURPLE SIDE
OF BLUE

O'NEIL DE NOUX

LaStanza backed away from the body, out of the police lights, and stepped up on the sidewalk. He wiped the sweat from his forehead and looked at his partner as she stood over the body. Detective Jodie Kintyre, in a white blouse and black slacks, her 9 mm in a shoulder rig, leaned over the body of a young woman lying in the center of narrow Coliseum Street next to the concrete ramp leading up to the Mississippi River Bridge.

Jodie's blond hair, cut in a pageboy, blocked her features as she leaned forward. A crime lab technician stood behind her, a large black camera dangling around his neck. He looked impatient.

LaStanza wrote a brief description of the victim in his notepad—white female, late twenties, wearing a red T-shirt, black shorts and white tennis shoes—Nike brand. He wouldn't even try to guess her height or weight in her crumpled state, figuring he'd get it at the autopsy.

Humidity, as thick as steam rising from a pot of boiled rice, made the night air heavy. Summer nights in New Orleans were always hot, always. Even after a long rain, the evening was especially steamy in the narrow confines of a one-lane street sandwiched between a concrete ramp and a four-story building. This particular street smelled of tar and oil and faintly of vomit.

LaStanza turned and looked at the building, at the old marquee in front. Its white paint was peeling, the "e" missing from atop the marquee, which marked the defunct movie house as the Coliseum Theater. A bus went up the ramp behind LaStanza, belching rancid exhaust in the stagnant air.

A blond-haired patrolman, wearing a name plate that identified him as R. Nelson, stepped up on the sidewalk next to LaStanza and said, "Wow. I've never seen a neck snapped like that."

He was young.

The patrolman went on. "Was she was thrown off the overpass, or what?"

Over six feet, R. Nelson was a good six inches taller than LaStanza, who ran his right hand through his thick dark hair, dabbed his mustache with his index finger and thumb. He did that often, when lost in thought.

LaStanza looked back at the body and said, "Or what."

"Huh? Oh," Nelson said. "Her neck's broke, isn't it?"

LaStanza looked up at the roof of the theater. He shined his flashlight on the stucco wall, also in dire need of paint. He loosened his red-and-silver tie as he walked around to the side of the theater.

He pressed his black Kel-Lite flashlight against a rusty wrought-iron gate and it creaked open. The grass was knee-high and thick alongside the theater, except for a recent-looking trail leading from the gate to the fire escape ladder that zigzagged up to the roof, with two small landings.

LaStanza went down on his haunches and saw the grass was recently trampled. He made his own fresh trail to the ladder and spotted grass and mud on the lower rungs of the ladder.

He moved back out to the sidewalk and called to Jodie, "I'm going up."

"What?" She shined her flashlight at him.

He pointed his light up the building and told her about the grass and mud on the ladder.

"For God's sake, be careful," Jodie said, waving the photographer forward.

"You want me to go with you?" It was Nelson again.

LaStanza pulled his portable radio from the back pocket of his blue suit pants and handed it to Nelson.

"Hold this, Ricky. I'll be right back down."

"My name's Ronald."

"Yeah. Right. Mind singing a few bars of 'Travelin' Man' as I go up?"

"What?"

"How old are you?"

"Twenty-two."

At thirty-five LaStanza didn't feel that old, but he was looking at a police officer who never even heard of Ricky Nelson. The summer of 1985 and the Teenage Idol was already gone and forgotten.

LaStanza moved over to the fire escape ladder and gave it a good shake. Bolted to the wall, it looked a lot newer than the gate and seemed solid. He made sure to not step on the grass and mud on the lower rungs on his way up. At the first landing, he slipped the flashlight into his back pocket and tried the door. Locked.

He used both hands on his way up to the second landing. The door was locked there too. The next stop was the roof. LaStanza took in a deep breath. The air still smelled of oil up high, the humidity just as thick. LaStanza wiped his damp hands on his pants and went up.

The roof was particularly dark. LaStanza pulled out his flashlight and flipped it on. Moving along the edge of the pitched roof, just inside the two-foot ledge, he found broken beer bottles, Coke cans, several worn tennis shoes, sheets of newspaper, a dead pigeon and a note taped to the ledge overlooking Coliseum Street. The note read:

Daddy,
I'm sorry. It hurts all the time. I can't take it.

I will love you forever,
Olivia

Police. I live at 1437 Euterpe. In the yellow house.

After copying the note verbatim in his small notepad, LaStanza took his time checking for drag marks or any signs of a struggle. Leaning over the ledge, he calculated she had to leap to clear the marquee to make sure she landed in the street. He inched to his left and spotted a blade of grass in some more mud where she must have stood before leaping.

He was dripping by the time he climbed down the ladder. He slid his flashlight back into his pants pocket and wiped the sweat from his arms before retrieving his radio from Nelson, who asked, "Find anything?"

"Just a note."

"A what?" Nelson followed LaStanza out to where Jodie stood. Her notepad in hand, Jodie jotted down the measurements called out by the technician who triangulated the exact location of the body in the street.

"Make sure he measures from the theater," LaStanza told her.

"Huh?"

"Then he needs to go up and photograph the note she left on the roof ledge before she jumped. And collect the grass and mud on the ladder and the ledge up top."

"What?" Jodie's wide-set cat eyes glowered at him.

LaStanza bent over and checked out the bottom of the victim's Nikes more closely. No grass, but mud still clung to the bottom of both shoes. Standing, he pulled out his notepad and read the transcription of the victim's note aloud.

Jodie looked at the marquee and then up at the roof. He could see the tension fall away from her pretty face. She was experienced enough to know suicide was just paperwork. Murder was work.

"No sign of a struggle?"

He shook his head.

Nelson slapped his knee and said, "Son of a gun. She jumped."

The crime lab technician didn't like having to take more pictures—of the body in relation to the theater. He didn't like triangulating more measurements, much less climbing up to the roof with his camera. But he was really pissed when he came down without the note and Jodie sent him right back up to get it.

"You think he's stupid enough to touch it?" she asked LaStanza when the technician started back up the ladder.

"In this city, anything's possible."

Jodie hurried over to the ladder and called up to the tech to make sure he secured the note without touching it so he could spray it later for prints. Jodie's voice echoed down Coliseum Street. Somewhere in the darkness, a dog barked in response.

LaStanza took Nelson with him to canvass the area, in case anyone saw anything. He wasn't optimistic. After midnight, the law-abiding citizens were locked in their houses behind shuttered windows. The only people usually out on the street were those who didn't like talking to police.

———

The canary-yellow, single-story shotgun house at 1437 Euterpe Street was four blocks from the Coliseum Theater. Like most shotgun houses, it was raised a few feet off the ground on brick pillars. Jodie led LaStanza up the three brick steps to its narrow front gallery. She rang the doorbell. LaStanza looked up at the gingerbread trim along the hipped roof above the gallery.

"Who's there?" a male voice called out from behind the white wooden door.

"Police," Jodie said.

The door opened and an old man peeked out at them. Jodie pointed to her gold star-and-crescent badge clipped to her belt and said, "I'm Detective Kintyre and my partner's Detective LaStanza."

The man turned his deep-set eyes toward LaStanza who added, "Homicide."

The old man leaned his wrinkled face forward. Recognition, like pinpricks, came to his eyes, his mouth curling into a frown. LaStanza figured he was in his late sixties. The door opened slowly and the man sagged. Jodie reached for him, but the old man held on to the door and shook his head.

The old man turned and moved though his living room, flipping on a brown lamp next to a tan sofa, moving to a side window to turn on the air conditioner before sinking back on the sofa. He closed his red-and-black plaid robe around his naked legs. He wore short, blue-striped pajamas and brown slippers. When he looked back at LaStanza, his eyes glistened.

The detectives waited, standing awkwardly in the small living room, thankful for the AC, the sweat drying on their backs and in their hair.

Blinking away tears, the old man said in a hollow voice, "Olivia's dead, isn't she?"

Jodie nodded.

"How?" His lower lip quivered.

"It appears to be a...suicide."

The old man took in a deep breath. He swallowed and waved for them to sit. Jodie sat in a matching tan sofa chair. LaStanza sat in the wooden rocker at the other end of the sofa.

"Joshua Logan," the old man said. "I'm Olivia's father." He closed his eyes and took in another deep breath. "She's with her mother now." He wiped his eyes with a spindly hand marked with brown age spots.

"I want you to tell me how she did it."

He spoke to LaStanza who pointed to Jodie and said, "It's her case, sir."

The old man looked at Jodie who told him about the theater and the note. Logan nodded as she spoke. When Jodie finished, Logan said Olivia had been up on the Coliseum Theater once before and thought about jumping. That was a couple months ago.

"Olivia had problems." Logan stared straight ahead at the wall across the room. "She was raped."

LaStanza felt a sinking in his stomach. He watched Jodie's face as the old man told the story.

Six years ago, when Olivia was fifteen a man grabbed her off the street, raped and beat her repeatedly in his car and threw her off the Camp Street ramp up to the Mississippi River Bridge, breaking her hip.

Jodie's wide-set cat eyes narrowed and she leaned forward to take notes, looking up with her jaw set.

"She never got better," Logan said of his daughter. "Her hip healed and the police, y'all caught the man, but she wasn't like the way she used to be." Logan took in another breath. "Her mama died of cancer last year and Olivia got worse. She quit work. She stayed in her room." He looked up at the ceiling.

"She used to be a happy girl."

That sentence caused Jodie to close her eyes momentarily. LaStanza rubbed his stomach, as if that would do any good.

"Then we got word the man got out of jail some months ago. Olivia pretended like it didn't matter, but it did. I tried to get her to go see a doctor, a psychiatrist or something, but she wouldn't go."

The old man's eyes teared up again and he wiped them with the sleeve of his robe. Jodie stood up suddenly and paced back and forth from her chair to LaStanza's and back. She didn't look at her partner as she walked back and forth. She looked at her notes.

LaStanza noticed an old picture in a silver frame. Joshua Logan stood next to a pretty, dark-skinned woman. They were both smiling.

"What's the man's name?" LaStanza asked, which brought both Logan and Jodie back.

"Leon Granches."

LaStanza and Jodie both wrote the name in their notes. Jodie asked Logan if they could see Olivia's room.

The old man nodded.

LaStanza asked Logan if he was going to be all right. The old man nodded again and pushed himself off the couch and led them back through his bedroom through another bedroom to a third bedroom with yellow wallpaper and needlepoint designs framed on the walls. Logan moved over to a cedar chifforobe and took a picture off it and passed it to Jodie.

"That was taken two years ago."

LaStanza looked around Jodie's shoulder. Olivia had her mother's dark complexion and her father's eyes, only they looked troubled, even when she smiled.

Logan sat on the double bed and put his right hand on a pillow and looked down at the pillow. LaStanza could see the old man mouthing words at the pillow.

Jodie moved around the room in slow motion, picking up a hairbrush momentarily, looking at the assortment of cosmetics atop the small ivory vanity. Finally, she put the picture back on the chifforobe and asked Mr. Logan if Olivia had kept a diary.

The old man shook his head.

Jodie dug a card out of her purse and put it in the old man's hand.

"If you think of anything else, call me." She took the card back momentarily and wrote a phone number on the back. "That's my home number."

Jodie started out of the room. LaStanza stepped up to the old man and told him to have whatever funeral home he decided on call the coroner's office tomorrow.

The old man's eyes were closed but he nodded.

LaStanza joined Jodie in the doorway just as the old man said, "Leon Granches killed her. When he raped her, he killed her back then."

The old man pulled his feet up on the bed and lay back on the pillow, draping his arm over his eyes. In a barely audible voice he said, "She used to be a happy girl."

———

LaStanza slipped a sheet of paper into the beat-up Smith-Corona typewriter atop his government-issue gray metal desk and added Olivia's vital stats to their daily report —white female, twenty-three, five feet two inches tall, 120-125 pounds. There wasn't much more to add. The autopsy that morning revealed the cause of death was a fractured skull and a broken neck. The manner of death—suicide.

He flipped off the typewriter and kicked his tired legs up on his desk. He looked at the wall of windows to his right, at the peeling green tint that gave the windows that leprosy look in the morning sunlight. He squinted at the bright light.

Turning, he looked at the clock on the wall, which hung above the unofficial logo of the Homicide Division—an art deco drawing of a vulture perched atop a gold NOPD star-and-crescent badge. It wasn't even ten thirty and he was beat.

He put his hands behind his head, settled back in his gray secretary's chair and closed his eyes.

He tried to catch a little sleep, but his eyes snapped open after a minute. It was just too quiet in the squad room, so quiet it was eerie. It happened only once a month, when the shifts rotated. And this was their first day on the day watch. He stood and stretched, reached into his desk drawer for the newest coffee mug his wife gave him—a black mug with a gold hangman's noose emblazoned on both sides.

He was just pouring himself a strong cup of coffee and chicory when Jodie came in. Shoving chairs, she kicked a trash can on her way to her desk where she slammed down her briefcase and sat heavily in her desk chair, and looked at the wall of leprosy windows.

"Want some coffee?"

"No!"

Figuring the last thing she needed was caffeine, LaStanza took his coffee to his desk and sat and watched his partner. Jodie ran her hands through her hair, drummed her fingers on her desk, folded her arms again and crossed her legs. In another white blouse, tan slacks, her 9 mm in a brown leather holster along her right hip, she looked as fresh and crisp on the outside as if she'd slept twelve hours. Her face was smooth, without the hint of a line or wrinkle. Then again, she was only twenty-five.

LaStanza loosened his black-and-gold tie and readjusted the new black canvas holster carrying his .357 Magnum on his right hip. He also wore tan today. He'd left his suit coat in the car, but his pants matched the color of Jodie's perfectly. He hated when they matched colors.

Someone was bound to say, "Don't they look cute?"

157

Jodie turned to him with her cat eyes like slits and said, "They're so damn stupid, it's ridiculous!" After the autopsy, Jodie had gone to the DA's office to talk to them about Leon Granches. That was an hour and a half ago.

LaStanza waited.

Jodie stood and leaned her right fist on her desk. "They let Granches plead to forcible rape. He got twenty years. After eight, he's out on parole. Damn, federal judges with their over-crowding rules!"

Her voice rose. "You should have heard them when I told them they let a murderer out after eight years. They got all goggle-eyed. 'He killed her,' I said. 'He killed her when he raped her. It just took her this long to die.' You know what they said?"

LaStanza could imagine.

"They said they didn't understand." Jodie waved her arms. "I'm standing in an office with three ADA's, two of them women, and they have this blank stare in their eyes."

"I begged them to let me go in front of the grand jury. Begged them. Rape kills! I can prove it." She slammed the palm of her hand down on her desk. "I can get an indictment!"

LaStanza nodded.

Jodie raised a fist. "He murdered her, the bastard!"

LaStanza opened his notepad and said, "Where is he now?"

"Huh?"

"Let's get his parole officer on the phone, find out where the lovely Mr. Granches is staying. I'm in the mood to fuck with a criminal." LaStanza felt the leopard stirring inside. He liked that.

There's an old saying in Homicide—don't think it can get worse, because it will.

LaStanza and Jodie, in their tan outfits, stood in the narrow sergeant's office of the Sex Crimes Unit, while Detective Sergeant Frank Savage told them how Leon Granches was one of many suspects in a new series of uptown rapes.

"He's living, of all places, across the street from Cohen High School." Savage shook his head, his short straight black hair barely moving. Pushing forty, Savage looked older, his lean face lined with premature wrinkles. "We've watched him on and off during this latest series of rapes but we can't watch everybody all the time."

No need to explain. Not only were they underpaid, but NOPD was horribly undermanned. The long blue line was drawn thin now, dangerously thin.

"Over the last three weeks," Savage said, "eight women have been raped by a white male using the same MO. He comes up behind them when they're going into their house or apartment, forces them in, rapes them, then makes them bathe. He takes the bedsheets and all the victim's clothes with him."

He's been handled before, LaStanza thought.

"He knows all about evidence," Savage said.

"Do you have a composite?" Jodie asked.

"He wears a ski mask." Savage covered his face with his hands and spoke through his fingers in a tired voice, "He fits Granches's general description, along with thirty-nine other known sex offenders living uptown."

Pulling his hands down, Savage reached into one of the trays on his government-issue gray metal desk and came out with a thick file. He found a mug shot of Leon Granches and passed it to Jodie. He read off Granches's address: 1823 Delachaise Street. LaStanza wrote it down while his partner looked at the mug shot.

"Whatever y'all have in mind is OK with me." The sides of Savage's thin mouth curled up. He looked at LaStanza and said, "I hope he's foolish enough to pull something on you. A knife. A fork. A spoon." Savage smiled a shark smile.

Jodie didn't seem to be listening. LaStanza shrugged and said, "So what's another grand jury, right?"

LaStanza had been there enough times. All good shootings, of course. Enough for people to talk behind his back and joke to his face.

Jodie passed LaStanza the mug shot, thanked Savage and led the way out. LaStanza followed.

From behind, Savage called out, "I like your matching outfits."

———————

Outside the "police only" elevator, Jodie said, "I want Granches."

"Fine. Let's nail him."

"I mean it," she said.

"So do I." He knew his voice didn't sound like it, but he meant it.

"He's a criminal. He's stupid. He'll make a mistake." She punctuated it by slapping the "down" button again.

Just as LaStanza and Jodie stepped into the elevator, their sergeant called them on the radio. Jodie answered while LaStanza looked at the flat, narrow face of Leon Granches. It was a plain face, with small eyes and a smaller than usual mouth.

LaStanza was immediately distracted by his sergeant's message. There was a double murder working at a barroom on Chef Menteur Highway.

"Gee, I love this city," LaStanza said.

———————

They finished booking the last suspect of the barroom killing at seven p.m. LaStanza was so tired, even his hair ached. For a change, Jodie looked beat as they climbed into their unmarked Ford LTD.

"Wanna swing by Granches's house?" He asked as he cranked up the engine.

Jodie nodded, smiled and said, "Yeah. Good idea."

It was on their way home, in a roundabout way. And LaStanza's wife was out of town for the week. *So,* LaStanza thought, *why not?*

"Mind if we pick up some burgers?" he said.

"Oh, definitely."

They swung by Wendy's on Saint Charles Avenue and took their burgers, fries, and frosty shakes over to Delachaise Street. It took two passes to spot Granches's house. They found it by eliminating the addresses on either side. Granches lived in a ramshackle, unpainted wooden house with a tin roof right across from the blond-brick Cohen Senior High School. Set back between two large magnolia trees, 1823 Delachaise was a shack. One of those concrete three-step things used on house trailers served as its front porch. A beat-up metal garbage can stood in front of the shack, between the broken sidewalk and the blacktop street.

"You think he's in there?"

"That window unit's running," LaStanza said, pointing his chin at the air conditioner dangling from a side window. "Let's eat."

They parked a half block down the street, beneath a large oak and rolled down the windows. They ate their suppers in silence. After the sun set, LaStanza settled against the driver's door and watched his partner's face in the yellow hue of the streetlights.

Jodie's jaw was tight, her lips pursed together as she watched Granches's shack. Her legs were crossed and her arms folded as she sat stiffly in her seat. She was wound way too tight.

This case was working her, instead of her working the case. This one would stick around. And there was nothing he could do about it but ride it out with his partner. Olivia would haunt Jodie. That happened sometimes. Some…no…many of LaStanza's victims still visited his thoughts. It was only human.

LaStanza stretched his legs and tried to get comfortable. Every time he moved, something ached. His eyes burned and when he blinked, his eyelids ached.

Jodie cleared her throat and said in a scratchy voice, "I feel like I've been beat up from the inside out." She was talking to the windshield. "I feel all bruised up inside."

"It's the pressure cooker," he told her again. He'd told her about the Homicide Pressure Cooker the first day.

"Yeah. Yeah." She was tired of hearing it.

The door of the shack opened and yellow light streamed out. Leon Granches, wearing only a pair of yellow gym shorts, took a large plastic garbage bag out to the garbage can and tossed it in. Turning back for his house, he spotted them. Ducking quickly, he hurried back inside.

"Let's go," LaStanza said, starting the LTD. Three seconds later, he pulled the key from the ignition and followed his partner up the three concrete trailer steps to the unpainted wooden door. Jodie used the butt of her portable radio to knock on the door. They stood on either side of the door, LaStanza's hand on the black rubber grip of his Smith & Wesson .357 Magnum model 66.

"Come on, Granches," Jodie said as she knocked again. "Open up."

The door rattled and Granches peeked out at them.

"Can we come in?" Jodie said, answering her own question just as quickly. "Thanks, don't mind if we do." She shoved the door in and Granches stepped back. LaStanza followed his partner into a cluttered living room with two brown sofas, a wooden coffee table covered with pizza boxes and beer cans, a lone lamp on a mismatched end table.

The room smelled of stale beer. The carpet was sticky. Leon Granches stood next to one of the sofas, his hands folded in front of his bare, hairless chest. He'd lost weight since the mug shot was taken. Over six feet tall, he probably didn't weigh 150.

As Jodie poked around the room, using her radio to touch things, LaStanza stepped up and looked Granches in the eyes. The pupils dilated, the white of his eyes were yellow.

"What are you on?" LaStanza asked.

"Nothin', man." Granches looked down at his feet. He shook as he stood, as if he was standing in his own private earthquake.

163

Jodie tapped LaStanza on the shoulder. He stepped aside as his partner stuck her face in Granches's face. "So, how're you doing Leon?"

He shrugged.

LaStanza had a gut feeling. The hair along the back of his neck stood up, and he was sure he heard the leopard growling low inside. Something was very wrong here.

While Jodie toyed with Granches's little mind, asking him how he found such a nice place, LaStanza started a meticulous search of the place, picking up dirty clothes, pulling the other sofa away from the wall. He moved into the kitchen area and saw Granches watching his every move.

"So, where you working, Leon?" Jodie asked.

"I work for Manpower." His mouth quivered.

"What's that?"

"I deliver flyers. Door to door."

Jesus! Somebody's sending a convicted rapist door to door!

LaStanza dodged the roaches in the kitchen. He didn't want to break up their meeting. The sink was filled with dirty dishes, so was the Formica table. More roaches there too.

LaStanza checked out the closet between the living room and the lone bedroom. Its narrow shelves were stuffed with clothes and shoes. He had trouble pulling out a large drawer at the bottom. It only opened a few inches. He saw a dirty sheet and left it. Granches was eyeballing him pretty closely now.

LaStanza found Granches's stash under his bed. As soon as he moved into the small bedroom, he smelled weed and spotted a couple reefer-roaches in the ash tray next to the bed. He found two lids of marijuana, a bottle full of different colored pills, and a bottle with several nice-sized chunks of crack in a plastic bag under the bed.

He carried the stuff out and dropped it atop one of the pizza boxes on the coffee table.

Jodie shook her head and said, "Looks like you're a parole violator, Leon."

Granches shrugged.

"Say Leon, you remember a girl named Olivia Logan?" Jodie said.

"Huh?" Leon looked at his feet again.

"Come on, you remember Olivia. You just served time for raping her. You remember now?"

Leon shook his head.

"That's why we're here, Leon. Olivia's dead." Jodie reached over and poked Leon on the sternum with the knuckles of her right hand. "You killed her Leon. And you're going to answer for it."

Leon's jaw dropped, and he looked at LaStanza who rubbed his own chest and said, "Hurts, doesn't it?"

Jodie poked Leon again, and he fell back on the sofa, his hands at his sides, his mouth still open.

LaStanza moved back to the closet and pulled on the drawer again. He had to yank it, but it finally opened. He brushed the sheet away and saw a face. Dull eyes pointing straight up, mouth open in the unmistakable look of death.

"Jesus!"

A crash behind LaStanza turned him around as Granches lunged from the sofa tripping on the coffee table. He tumbled to the sticky carpet. Jodie jumped on him a second before LaStanza landed on his skinny legs.

Granches squirmed and tried to hit Jodie, but she pinned

his right arm down and punched him in the throat. He howled when LaStanza twisted his left arm back and slapped a handcuff on his wrist.

LaStanza grabbed the right arm, yanked it back, cuffed it, then stood up like a rodeo cowboy who just finished tying up a steer. He helped Jodie to her feet. Granches cried as he lay at their feet, a touch of blood on his lips.

"What the hell was all that?" Jodie said when she regained her breath.

"Take a look in the closet." LaStanza's voice was low and even, his heartbeat already leveled off. It was a Sicilian trait. When others lose their heads, keep yours and you'll live longer.

Jodie let out a long low-pitched moan when she looked down into the drawer. She moved slowly back to the men, pointed to Granches and said, "We shouldn't have cuffed him. Now we can't shoot him."

"Yes we can." LaStanza looked at Granches's tiny eyes. "We just take the cuffs off after." He felt the leopard again, incensed by the smell of blood.

Jodie took LaStanza's arm and pulled him to the other side of the room and whispered in his ear, "How're we gonna work this?"

Still eyeballing Granches, LaStanza spoke softly. "Easy. He waved us over, invited us in and said he had something to show us." He looked at his partner's wide eyes. "It's his word against ours. Who they gonna believe?" He pointed to the closet, "He's got a fuckin' head in a drawer!"

———

A pair of second district officers arrived first. LaStanza had them guard the door. Ten minutes later, Sergeant Mark Land pulled up. In a rumpled white dress shirt, baggy jeans, and tennis shoes, Mark filled the doorway. He looked like as big as a grizzly. He glared at Granches, still lying on the floor, looked up at LaStanza and Jodie with a scowl.

Taller and much thicker than LaStanza, with a nearly identical thick mustache and unruly brown hair, Mark could pass for LaStanza's older brother. He went into his bear impersonation, huffing his favorite obscenities as he crossed the room to tower over LaStanza, who pointed to the closet.

With his brow furrowed, Mark cursed his way over to the closet, looked in the drawer and shut up. He shut up. He leaned forward for a closer look, pulled back and walked over to Granches to stand over him a moment.

Granches started crying again, and Mark turned away with a sarcastic, pained look on his face. He moved back to Jodie and LaStanza. He stuck his hands in his back pockets and motioned toward the closet with his head and said, "That's something you don't see every day."

LaStanza nodded. Jodie was expressionless. LaStanza saw it again, in her face, the pressure. Mark's lame joke relieved none of the pressure.

"Um." Mark raised his hand and spoke carefully, pronouncing each word one at a time. "How in the hell did y'all do this?"

LaStanza was going to tell him it was good police work, but opted for their prepared story. "He waved us over, invited us in and said he had something to show us." LaStanza dabbed his mustache with his index finger and thumb.

Jodie huffed and moved back to the closet. She leaned against the doorframe and looked down in the drawer.

Mark started rubbing his temples and asked, "Why were y'all here?"

"Oh." LaStanza told him about Olivia and the Coliseum Theater and the old man in the yellow house and about how Granches got off after serving eight years and how Jodie and he planned to be all over Granches like beans on rice until they caught him at something.

He wasn't sure which part Mark didn't believe, but was sure Mark believed enough that LaStanza's story would work. "Just ask Jodie."

Frank Savage came in just in front of the crime lab technician. Mark Land had pulled his notepad from his coat pocket and had taken over. Savage tiptoed past Mark and walked up to LaStanza.

"So y'all got Granches, huh?"

LaStanza nodded.

"I just came to tell you we caught the uptown rapist an hour ago." He shrugged, "At least the guy we caught was using the same MO."

"Another paroled sex criminal?"

"How'd you guess?" Savage pointed to Jodie, and LaStanza told him to go take a look. He did and came back rubbing his lean chin. He folded his arms, looked back at Jodie and asked how in the hell did they solve this one.

"Matching outfits," LaStanza said, pointing to his pants and then his partner's slacks as he moved over to stand next to her.

Jodie tilted her chin toward him and said, "I see things like this and know it's real, but it's so unreal."

He let her talk it out.

"I wonder who she was. Where she lived? What school she went to?" Jodie took in a deep breath. "I wonder what could have brought a young woman to end up like this?"

"A federal judge."

Jodie rubbed her eyes with her fingertips. "I feel so beat up." She stopped rubbing her eyes but kept them closed. "I feel all bruised inside."

LaStanza knew the feeling.

Paul Snowood chose that moment to come in. Wearing a black cowboy hat, a leather vest over a denim shirt and jeans and snakeskin boots, Country-Ass said, "There's a passel o' dogs trying to get in that garbage can outside."

LaStanza and Jodie looked at one another and headed straight out.

Granches cried louder and Mark told him to shut the fuck up.

Retrieving their flashlights from their car, LaStanza and Jodie carefully untied the twist tie atop the black garbage bag and opened it. A bloody dress was wrapped around a woman's leg.

"Jesus Fuckin' Christ!"

Mark came out to look, asked if they were up to interviewing Granches. No matter how many body parts they found, the only way to get the DA to go for a touchdown was with a confession.

"He'll talk to me," Jodie said through gritted teeth.

LaStanza figured she'd want that interview and smiled coldly.

THE REMARKABLE WAY SHE DIED

KAREN FONVILLE

Professional writer Karen Fonville, in her first story in *Pulphouse*, made a funeral come alive like no funeral you have ever seen. You will not soon forget this funeral, and in a good way.

Karen tends to write a lot of mystery and detective short stories which I love. For now, enjoy the funeral.

THE REMARKABLE WAY SHE DIED

KAREN FONVILLE

MARTY

There wasn't a dry eye in the house at Sally June's funeral. And it was the noisiest funeral I ever did see.

But it sure was pretty.

Sally June was in her very best Sunday dress, all blue with white flowers on it, lace around the sleeves and a white apron tied around her waist. She might not have liked that apron, but she wore it proud. It's something she worked really hard for.

Her red hair was long and the mortician had brought it down over her shoulders, just like she wore it that last day. He even put the pretty brown hair combs in her hair...those ones with the rhinestones. They sparkled in the light that shone on her. The light was harsh, but it made her look pretty.

But we can't see her blue eyes.

That funeral home was mighty fancy, too. The chairs, folding-style, sure, but they had cushions on the seats. And those

173

cushions were blue velvet like. The carpet on the floor was thinner than I like, but it was blue like the cushions, the corn-flower blue that matched Sally June's eyes.

The casket, copper-colored, shoned in the light, looked just as good as any of them others, with its cream-colored lining that brought out her freckles even through the heavy pancake makeup they put on her.

You can't even see the scars.

That's very good work.

Now, they none of them thought anyone'd come see to Sally June, so they started her out in a tiny room off to the side. But even before the first of us got there, they'd had to move her to the big room.

Too many flowers came. Oh, the big, big, big flower arrangements. Lilies and such. Must a been 'bout fifty of them things. And the little un's too, the tiny planters that some people take home and try to keep the memories alive.

That's a real shame. Ain't nobody that knows her real well that can take one of them planter things. But that's neither here nor there. They's a beautiful sight all crowded there down the front. An I reckon it's the thought that counts.

Sure, coulda used some of that money for food, though. Sorry, shouldn'ta said that, it's just I'm so darn hongry.

But to get back to it, that big room filled up so full, Sally June woulda had to leave if'n she was alive. That wonderful woman couldna stand too many people in one place. And this would sure have set her off.

Those nice purty cornflower-blue curtains that divided this room from that smaller room had to be pulled back, an it still weren't enuff room. All of us what travelled with Sally June, we'd stood along the walls and crouched when there was room, so's the big guns could get in.

You know, the mayor and council, the Ladies' Auxiliary, the biggest church choir that ever sang off-key. Musta been very hot up there when that one lady fainted. I tried hard not to laugh when she took out the three rows in front of her. Thought I covered it with a cough, but Montana Joe, looking strange without his favorite rope curled over his shoulder, says he heered it plain, so maybe not.

SALLY JUNE

I didn't mean to die that day.

Really, I didn't.

I'm Sally June Riddell, and you won't believe what happened to me.

Right now, though, I'm laying here in the copper casket, watching all these people in their Sunday finest come in to see me off. None of these'n's are who I want to see.

They're here, though. I knows cause I can smell 'em. That there lavendar Old Spice, that's Marty K. Never could teach him how to use that body wash. Thinks it's cologne.

And Petey, well, poor man chews garlic any chance he gets.

That stupid mortician, couldn't put my hair up on my head to make me pretty. Had to keep that gosh-darn red hair lying on my shoulders, pulling all the color from my face. BAH! Shoulda had a lady do me up right. And I want to know who put this gal-darn white apron on me. Have you *ever* heard of a soman being buried in an *apron*?

The stink of these funeral flowers is just about enough to

wake the dead. Most of them are so pale, they're not even pretty. The ribbons are, but I can't see very many of those.

My nose itches something awful, and my eyes itch, too. I know, you're not supposed to feel nothing when you're dead. I cain't explain it. They itch.

The ceiling's kinda pretty, what I can see of it. It's vaulted, which I guess is supposed to help with the heat.

That's not working. I can feel the pancake makeup melting right off me. If they don't hurry and get me in the ground this goop is gonna ruin my best dress. At least the fellas got that right.

Thank goodness I ain't gonna have to walk outta here. I don't think they put any undies on me!

A bit of my mind keeps wandering back to that day. Trying to figure out something else I coulda done so I wouldn't' be in this mess. I'd be riding on out of here on the Western Southern Railroad, headed for the sun.

But I ain't. And the only riding I'm doing from now on is to the grave.

Some fool starts yammering. Then some ladies start cater-wauling.

Then there's a big commotion. Screams and thuds and more thuds.

I hear Marty K. cackling over behind my head some-where's and I wish could see what's going on. Must be some-thing right special. He ain't laughed in years.

MARTY

I had to turn around, face the wall. Tears flooding down my cheeks, and I know them cheeks is turning purple with trying to stop laughing. But all them high falooting ladies going ass over teakettle were just about the funniest thing I ever seed.

Montana Joe rushed into the fray to help them ladies up. It's possible he helped himself to a few of those ladies' purties. Sure hope not. That ain't respectable to our Sally June.

Man, I wish she coulda see'd the commotion.

I wish she hadn't died.

Maybe things ain't as funny as I'm makin' out. I reach inta my pocket for my kerchief.

Something falls to the ground while I dab my face. Won't do to have the boys see me blubber like a baby.

Montana Joe's back and he starts to reach for what fell ta the floor, then stops like it's a snake what would bite 'im. Looks at me, eyes wide and fillin'.

"A *marriage license?*"

SALLY JUNE

Gol darn that Marty K. I never told him yes. Montana Joe was just up here helping them fancy ladies (I just know he thought they wasn't wearing nothing under them fancy choir robes, but I don't think he got to see nothin'.) He's got a bad limp from where he jumped wrong off the train that time back in Denver. And it was pretty slow going back to his place behind my head, so he's got to be pretty disappointed.

Or maybe the locals just didn't want him messing with their women.

Anyway, that was his horrified whisper just now.

I heered 'marriage license' just fine. I tole that fool to wait. I ain't ready. Marty asked why not. I cain't tell him I's still married. Cain't tell nobuddy. He'd kill me.

The thought stops me cold.

Oh, wait.

Well, gol darn it! Too late for that, too!

I try to sit up so's I c'n shout it from the rafters, then I 'member. I's well and truly dead this time. And he did it.

MARTY

I hit Montana Joe in the side with my elbow. "Hush, fool. You're making a scene."

Must nota been ready, cause Montana Joe went down. I swear I didn't mean it. Grabbed up that paper and jammed it in my pocket, never turning back toward the altar again.

At the front, none of them ladies got hurt, so they's stand up again and start to sing Sally June's favorite hymn, "In the Garden."

And that's when it hit me.

She died because of that damn garden.

SALLY JUNE

I nearly gagged.

They were singing that song. Used to be my favorite song in the world. How I wished, dear Lord, that they'd sing something else. Somethin' peppy, like "I'll Fly Away!" Way I's understand it, going to the Promised Land's s'poosed to be joyful.

I ain't no saint. Never said I was. Never wanted this kinda shindig to send me off.

Not real proud of all I done the last fifteen years, but ya do what ya gotta to get by. An' I did the best I could. Took to the rails, to get away, always meant to settle down somewhere's but wan't sure I ever got far enuff away. So's I kept going.

I's not the best-lookin' woman in the bunch neither. An after being with Bill Riddell for twenty years, didn't want to never be with another. Still got the scars from that pig.

Oh, he was a pretty one, that Bill Riddell, and a sweet talker. Things didn't go sour with him for a long time. Thought we had a good marriage.

Nope it was just for show.

Pa gave him a job on the ranch, and he was good at the rustlin'. And slick. No one ever cast a side eye at the Bar None Ranch.

Leastwise not then.

I did the cookin' for the crew then. And the doctorin' lessen it was too bad. Knew there was some rustlin' goin on...not that other stuff though.

MARTY

We'd stopped in this town 'bout three days ago, Sally June, Montana Joe, Petey and 'bout ten others. Camped out down to the hobo junction and came to town to find work. All of us was tapped out, and the food was running low.

Mostly a small cow town, with ranches and a few farms lying out aways. Deep in the heart of Texas high country, so's not a lot of other towns anywheres about.

Sally June went to the Sunset Diner, offerin' to cook for em, but they shooed her outa there. Didn't make no sense, Sally June'd cleaned up down to the creek and looked mighty fine with her gray dress and the white apron, her red hair flowing free. Guess they could tell she was a hobo.

Some lady, think she was the preacher's wife, asked her to stop by. Said she needed some help cooking for a big party. Sally June could fix some dishes so's the lady could decide.

Sally June loved her some cooking, and did her best for the lady. But somethin' happened. When Sally June got back to camp, she was a changed woman. Pale, and trembling. I asked her what was wrong.

Started talking 'bout that lady's garden, mumbling under her breath. Didn't make no sense. Said it used to be hers.

I ain't never seen Sally June so riled up, not even when townies were roustin' us hobos in the dead of night.

I got hired at the stables, two bits a night. Montana Joe had a friend at a local ranch, hired on to fix some fences. None of us got permanent jobs, just for long enough to make a bit of eating money afore we headed on. Nothing differnt than we'd done most places.

Pete, well, he's a special case. He gets a job in purt near the biggest bank in every town we stop in. Not sure what he does, but after they check with previous banks, they almost always roll out the red carpet for him. Then, just like the rest of us, he works awhile afore moving on. And they's always sorry to see him go.

Just boggles the mind.

So's anyways, we tell Sally June not to mind nothing. She didn't have to work, we'd bring enough to spot her until next time if need be.

And then the fireworks started.

SALLY JUNE

I try to take deep breaths to calm down, but acourse I'm sitting here in this gal-darn copper coffin which isn't wide enough to move my arms. It twern't made for a woman to breathe in, let alone move around.

So's I close my eyes and think.

How'd I get here?

Well, when we pulled inta town, I knew we'd made a big mistake. Bumbledon, Texas, on the Bumble River.

Right back where I started from.

My grampa started the town, nigh onto sixty year ago, 'bout twenty years after the War Between the States ended. His cattle ranch was the biggest for awhile, until Bill Riddell got ahold of it.

Pa's biggest disappointment was not having a son, but Ma died within three years of birthing me. Oh, he raised me right. But Pa never married again. Said it just took the heart out of him when she left him. Told me I was the apple of his eye.

The ranch house wasn't big as things go. Rooms for him and me, for eating and sitting. Then the bunk house, the stables, the corrals. Grampa's original one-room log cabin up in them hills. Our riches were all in the cattle and the land. Not in possessions.

But Grampa took care of the town. And Pa did after that. Making sure the families were safe. Getting a school teacher in for the kiddies when there were more than three of us. Bringing in merchants to supply what we couldn't make our own selves.

And making sure that the railway came through here so that ranchers from near and far would bring their cattle to market. The town blossomed just enough to make it not so lonely.

The ladies from back east brought silly flowers and gardens. They brought dresses and shawls. And manners.

All I'd ever had was breeches until then. Guess Pa couldn't figure out how to clothe a young girl excepting as a boy. My hair was short as a boy's, too, so's it could hold a hat proper in the hot sun.

I worked from sunup to sundown with my pa. Riding the range, mending fences. I learned it all, and Pa was proud. Knew I'd make a good forewoman of the ranch after he was gone.

The town ladies got together, though, and told Pa in no uncertain terms it weren't good for me to gallavant like a man. Said I had to learn manners. Or I wouldn't find a man of my own.

MARTY

I never seed Sally June so riled up. She plum forgot what our plan was. Started screaming 'bout some man named Bill Riddell, no good low down varmint no good for anythin' except being shot.

That twere the fust time any of us even heered bout this Riddell fellow. I know. All the boys asked me who he was and I hadda shrug. "Ain't heered no more than you, Montana Joe. He must be some relation, though, with the same last name and all."

Sally June took off, walking fast enough I nearly had to run to catch up. Then I had to duck when she took a swing at me.

Glad I ducked when I did, she'd a decked me. Knock me out fer sure.

I sure heered the wind whistling as her closed fist passed right over my head.

"Sally June, where's ya going?"

She glared into my eyes, and ifn I'd been paper I'd a caught fire. Took a step back. Couldn't tell if the sweat running down my back came from her heat or from the leftover sun heat. My throat went dry, and I coughed.

"Don't ya be following me, Marty. I got some things to work out in my own head. I'll be back after a while. Ya'll are big enough to care for yourselves for a bit."

Sally June marched down the dry dusty dirt road, kicking up brown dust that covered her gray muslin dress. Her red hair blew in the wind, and along the way, she ripped that white apron off and dropped it behind her.

SALLY JUNE

Mrs. Owens is a lean woman with beautiful brown hair pulled into a snood, and warm eyes that I bet smile all the time. There was kindness in them eyes, and a serenity you don't see to much of in today's world. She had asked me to cook her a few dishes so's she could see ifn she wanted me to cook for her party.

Turned out the mayor's daughter, Penny Franklin, was getting betrothed. The mayor wanted a big todo at the church.

His wife wanted it to be a "society" todo. After all, their daughter was going to marry the next governor of Texas.

"Good for her," I said. "Many blessings on the union, I'm sure."

Mr. Owens was the pastor of the First Bumble Church, and had built his own home. A simple one-story white clapboard house, where the kitchen and dining room were the best features. Mrs. Owens gave me a quick tour before showing me to the kitchen. The parlor was nice size with a paisley couch and two highback chairs done in a pale blue fabric, all situated in front of the fireplace. On either side of the fireplace was a bookshelf.

Mostly religious books, I'd imagine, all in their brown and black binders.

There was a chill in the house, and Mrs. Owen hurried into the kitchen. There the walls were whitewashed, and a water-pump stood at the sink. The woodstove with burners sat near the back door, and a big box of split wood rested nearby.

There was an icebox in a closet behind the back door. A dining table and plenty of counter space to work on. Cabinets rose, and a handmade buffet carried actual porcelain china with beautiful pink roses decorating it.

"Ma'am, my food's gonna be just fine for this party, but please don't make me use that china. I'm likely to break it."

"Miss Sally June, don't you worry about that," Mrs. Owens said. "Penny's bridesmaids will be helping with the serving." She beamed. "How does the kitchen stack up? Will it do?"

"Yes'm, it's a right nice setup you've got here."

She offered coffee, and we talked business while we waited for it to heat up. We were just about done when Mr. Owens walked in from the church next door.

"Pastor Owens, I'd like you to meet Miss Sally June. She'll be back tomorrow to fix us some dishes that we might want to serve at the betrothal party next week. We can make a decision, and then get our supplies."

Pastor Owens didn't look like many preachers I'd ever known. He had smile lines, and kind blue eyes. His brown hair was a bit long, and there was an unruly curl that kept popping into his face. Looking at the two of them, I got the feeling that they were happy together, and that they were both quite a bit younger than I am.

That didn't bother me none. I'm no spring chicken anymore. Just glad my hair ain't faded none.

And that's when it happened.

Mrs. Owens offered to show me her garden.

I just love a good garden. Had me a fine one out to the ranch, before I left. Lots of purty roses and a whole passel of herbs that took *just* the right amount of water. I'd gone to the river with the wagon ever day, cause our old pump just couldn't bring up enuff water.

Filled two barrels for that garden, along with my other duties.

So, I loved me a good garden, and followed the preacher's wife willingly. And nearly died.

MARTY

Picked up that apron and followed Sally June, I did. Right to the graveyard. This un didn't have no fence. Not much special about it. Mostly wooden markers, a few stone ones, and some that fell over.

Oh, she never knew I was there. Hanging back about the length of a cornfield, I just barely kept her in sight.

Until she found one of them stone markers, and dropped down on a grave. Marcus Winchester.

Sally June sat there for a long time, just talkin' to herself.

185

Or maybe talking to the dead man. I don't know. All I know is that using that language, Sally June sure wan't talking to th' good Lord God Almighty.

Her face turned all shades o' red, and tears ran down her face. After some time, she began pounding on the ground.

Hated to do it, but she'd skin me alive if'n she caught me listenin' in.

SALLY JUNE

It was like twenty years of my life just faded away. That garden was set up just like my garden out at the ranch. The pretty roses, a pink that I'd only ever seen on my trellis, climbed in an arch framing the back door. Pink, like the barest blush of a dawn morning right after a pouring rain the night before.

Ma brought her rose start with her from back east when she married my pa. Ain't no one in this world had a right to them roses. No one but me.

And there's the trellis, itself. Pa built it for Ma. His special mark hidden there in the carved flowery parts.

Bluebells and some kinda yeller flowers in neat beds lined a walkway that meandered throughout the back yard, ending in the vegetable garden with a large box elder maple tree in the center. That tree was mighty tall, with a rounded top, and a wide swing hanging from a limb that stood at least fifteen feet off the ground. And just beyond the garden, a small creek trickled by.

As the sun sat, bullfrogs croaked.

Anger flushed through me, bright and hot. Nearly burst

the top of my head plum off. Took all my strength to wrangle it back into place afore I could speak.

"Where did ya get my garden?" The words, hot and bitter, startled Mrs. Owens. She backed away from me, eyes alight with fear.

"I'm sorry, ma'am," I muttered, turning away. "Didn't mean to make ye afeared of me."

Gently, I rubbed the whitewashed trellis where Pa had carved his name. "T'was my pa that made this trellis. I'd reckonize it anywhere. And my ma brought these roses with her when she came here."

That Mrs. Owens, she's a peach of a lady. Here, I'd skeered her somethin' fierce, and yet the light of compassion shone in them eyes. She reached my arm, and gave a gentle squeeze.

"Why, the man that's marrying young Penny donated that to us from his own house. Said he just knew the Lord wanted us to have it. And he's been such a blessing to the town. Why, he's going to make sure we get tourists here now that the cattle industry has faded. That way the railway won't leave."

"'Scuse me? We talking Bill Riddell here? Ain't he just 'bout old enuff to be that gal's grandpappy?"

The gentle lady blushed. "Well, that is true, but..." and here she leaned forward conspiratorially "...the match does seem one of love."

MARTY

I shouldn'ta left her there. We'd talked marriage, that's true. And I shoulda stayed with her. Sometimes, the better part of a marriage is knowing when to leave well enuff alone.

So, I headed back to town. Stopped by that preacher man's house to talk to the missus.

Cain't git it through my head. Sally June was still married. And she nairy said a word. I felt lower than a skunk. My woman musta had reasons.

Oh, the preacher's wife was in a fine fettle. Rushing around calling for the preacher. Said the town was gonna haf to get him (Riddle). I could see the whites of her eyes, she was so upset.

When I asked about Sally June, Mrs. Owens just moaned. "That poor woman. No wonder she ran away. None of us can blame her, after the way that man treated her. And when I told her Bill's plan for the town, she just rose up and ran out the door. I do hope she'll be all right."

When the preacher man walked into the house, I skedaddled with thanks to the missus. Lots of bowing my head as I left, too.

Sally June *knew*.

SALLY JUNE

I yelled and screamed at Pa, sitting there in the graveyard facing his grave. How could he have left me? I've been asking that for the last twenty years. And not just 'cause he died. Pa'd been in the pink of health. Doc said it were heart attack.

Mebbe 'twas.

Now, I'm wondering.

Bill haint never hit me afore Pa died. Oh, he'd been mad. We both been mad. And our fights were near to raising the roof.

But that man never raised a fist to me. Until Pa died.

For a time, the ranch continued on the way it was, now with the men asking *me* for orders. And I gave them. Atter all, I'd worked the land with them afore I got married.

Slowly, the men stopped coming to me. And Bill's beatings got worse and nearly ever day. Seemed like alls I had to do was breathe to make him hit me.

That's when I learnt 'bout the rustling. I tried to stop it. They men's stealing from our neighbors. And some of them didn't have much to start with. I tried to put my foot down.

That time he beat me about the face, left these nasty scars, broke a couple teeth and even a rib. That rib took a while to heal. It meant I couldn't fill the water barrels to water the garden. My roses, those beautiful pink teacup roses trailing up the trellis, faded and wilted. The tomatoes grew, but only one or two on a vine, and they were sickly pale green, not the bright green of other years. And man they was hard. The lettuce heads were puny and yellow, the green beans just up and died.

The garden failing was all my fault. Bill had to assign one of the men to tend the garden while my rib healed up. Charlie was his name. That man was short, and his clothes hung off him. Greasy hair flopped in his face, and food always hung in his mustache.

And his rheumy blue eyes stared at me whenever he was near. Gave me the heebee jeebies, I'm here to tell ya. I took to staying inside if he was about. Closed up the winders, too, so I wouldn't hear him with his tuneless whistle. Even in the heat of the day.

It got so bad, I had trouble sleeping.

One day I snuck outa the house, just to run down to the creek. Wanted to splash a little water on my head. Maybe sneak a nap unner the bushes round that Box Elder Maple tree.

There were voices just around the bend of the trail, and I stopped, hiding in the middle of the bushes, wishing I'd thought to wear my grey dress instead of this white one.

Bill and Charlie.

"When I'm ready, you can have her, but not before, Charlie. And then I don't wanna know what you do with her, you hear?"

Cold ran down my spine. My loving hubband giving me away?

And to that nasty Charlie? Who just stood there drooling and smacking his lips with a leering grin?

Somehow I got away afore his time came.

So, you see, when Mrs. Owens told me that pretty little Penny was marrying my man, I just had to do something.

MARTY

Sally June had to know that I meant business with my proposal. So I went to the courthouse and got a marriage license. Clerk said it was good fer a year, and I figgered it'd take that long for the divorce to come through. If'n she married me or not, Sally June would know I'd stand with her.

The clerk looked funny at me as he handed me the license. Asked was she any relation of Bill Riddell, the next governor.

The next governor?

Mouth hanging open, I shook my head. "Cain't rightly say, friend." That no good varmint weren't good enuff for my Sally June.

Marriage license in my pocket, I headed back to the cementury and Sally June. She waint there. Course.

SALLY JUNE

Wore myself out shouting and screaming at Pa's grave. Don't know how long I sat there watching the wind playing with the cat o'nine tails just peeking over the tiny ridge.

Don't know how much longer it took afore the sound sank inter my brain. Dry crispy rasping. Like dried cornstalks after harvest. Or the tall meadow grasses in a drought.

Wiping my tears on my dress, I rose and wandered that way.

The creek was dry. Everything that depended on lots of water was dying. I stared at the dry cracked creek bed, and felt like I was sliding down a steep cliff.

That creek ran past my old ranch house. It ran through the graveyard, and then to town. Town had water yestiddy.

Did it now? Tweren't none here.

I headed off cross country. It'd be just like that varmint to dam up the creek and not tell nobody.

MARTY

Rounded up the guys from the hobo camp, tole 'em we had to find Sally June. Pete handed out samiches and we sent them out in all directions.

Heading back to the graveyard, I came upon a mob o'men from the town, all in an uproar about that Bill Riddell. Told 'em 'bout Sally June being missing and a roar went up from them.

Seems Mr. Owens filled them in about Sally June's misfortune when she lived here afore. Seems some o'them same men helped search for her when she went missing afore. Now, with more insight, they saw red.

"Get Bill Riddell!" the men screamed as they flowed down the road toward the graveyard.

I had no idee his ranch was beyond that cementury. Lucky me got swept along.

Some of them town's men were hunters. Though Sally June weren't there, they found her tracks in the dry dusty creek bed.

That tweren't somethin they were expecting to see, either. That dry creek. Someone said to Pastor Owens, "She's headed cross country and upstream."

Them men followed her like they's bloodhounds their own selves. I ain't used to running, so's I was trailing behind a bit when they got to the dam running acrost the creek.

I ain't no expert, but it looked to me like a beaver dam that someone poured clay over. Alls I knows is that Sally June was standing in the middle of the dry bed, poking at that thing with a big stick.

She'd been at it for a bit, that was for sure. A big crack in that brown clay stuff ran about halfway up the ten feet of the dam. At the top was more sticks woven together, like someone was trying to make the dam taller.

"Hey, missy! Get out of there!"

I think that was the sheriff, out in front yelling at her. Some of the other men yelled at him, trying to tell him what was what. He tweren't having none of it.

"Toss me a rope," Sally June yelled, reaching into the crack and yanking on a stick. "We gotta tear this thing down. Or the town's gonna die."

The sheriff went official on my gal. "Young lady, this land belongs to Bill Riddell and if he wants to dam up his creek, he can."

I've never seen Sally June flare up like that. She marched right out of that creek bed and got in the sheriff's face. "My name is Sally June Riddell, daughter of Marcus Winchester. I'm here to tell you, this land is mine. Handed down to me by my father, who's resting in that graveyard yonder. I don't care what Bill Riddell has told you folks, I ain't dead. And I ain't gonna let him kill off the town that my grandpappy and my pa took good care of all their lives."

The sheriff, a middle-aged man with gray hair and a pot belly, gave way, his face running red in the fading sunlight.

By that time, a number of townsmen were down in the creek bed, hammering away at that clay and pulling at the sticks and logs that made up the main part of the dam.

Montana Joe and the rest of our crew showed up right as the fireworks between Sally June and the sheriff started. Montana Joe started pushing through the crowd, with his favorite rope curled around his shoulder.

Sally caught sight of him, and shouted with glee. "Joe! You brought your rope!"

As he made it to her side, his broad, toothless grin lit up his face. "Ain't never leave home without it, Sally June. You know that!" In one smooth motion, he whipped it off his shoulder and handed it to her.

Sally June made her way back to the dam, scrambling down the side of the creek. Slipping once, she ignored the shouts from the men above her. Her opening in the dam had been widened by others, leaving several large logs exposed. It took her all of thirty seconds to decide on the most crucial log, and she wrapped one end of the rope around the log, tying a hitch knot as tight as she could.

Then, she handed the end to Montana Joe. "Head to the top and pull, Joe. Get everyone to yank on this. I'll keep pounding away trying to free this log totally from the clay."

"No, ma'am, I ain't a gonna leave you." Joe stood his ground until she pushed him.

"I promise you, at the first sign that the log is moving, I will get out of the way." Sally June stated firmly.

Montana Joe shook his head, and started back.

My Sally June turned back to her task, as I finally reached Joe and pulled him to the top. Within a few minutes, we had our pulling crew set up, and Sally June gave us the countdown.

"One, two, three, *pull!*"

Nothing happened.

"One, two, three, pull!" she shouted again.

Nothing happened.

The sun was almost gone, and it was getting hard to see what was going on, down in the creek bed.

Sally June's strong alto voice floated on the slight breeze.

"One, two, three, pull!!!"

Once again, we pulled, straining with all our might.

We pulled so very hard, we were each almost laying in the next fellow's lap.

With a loud snap, the rope went slack. Montana Joe fell into me, I fell into the guy behind me and soon the whole line was down on the ground, holding a limp hemp rope and looking stunned.

Grunts and groans ran the entire length of the crew as we each scrambled to get free.

A low rumbling started, mixed with the sharp raps of logs and sticks hitting with each other.

We rose to our feet, and felt more than saw the massive logs break apart and begin to roll downstream rapidly. Water gushed and sprang into the air, coating us all with blessed coolness.

Fifty men cheering echoed across the field and back from the hills not too far away. Back slapping and hearty congratulations went on for at least fifteen minutes. I moved along the creek, looking for my Sally June.

I cain't find her.

Her body washed inter town the next morning. Bruises and broken bones say she couldn't get outta the way in time.

Them townies set us all up nice for the funeral, begged us to stay. Alls we want is Bill Riddell to get his due for what he did ta my girl.

Now that he's a "free man," aint no decent woman'd have him. Oncet word got out 'bout what he did to Sally June, and how he tried to hornswoggle the whole town, well, he aint going to Austin anytime soon, neither.

Mr. Owens, the preacher man, was so tore up, he couldn't preach the service, so they's got a traveling preacher man to preach.

We buried Sally June next to her pa and her ma. I thought about staying to town, but that train's a callin' my name.

I still carry the marriage license to mind me of her.

THE STEAM-MAN'S PLANTATION

J. STEVEN YORK

J. Steven York is a master at writing some of the most twisted and thoughtful stories being published. In this novelette, he gives us an amazing story of clockwork men in a world all their own.

Steve has been publishing novels and powerful short fiction for over thirty years now, and before that he worked writing in the gaming industry. Steve is also doing a really fun and off-the-wall internet comic, one of which he has allowed me to put in each issue on the back page.

THE STEAM-MAN'S PLANTATION

J. STEVEN YORK

"What do you want, Liberty Brass?" said the tin-man's voice from over my shoulder. "Where are you taking me?"

I urged my clockwork horse, Piston, on into the morning fog without a look back. For now, this trouble-maker, Rusty Jack, wasn't going anywhere I didn't take him. And he wouldn't be shooting anyone else for some time to come. I knew he'd stay right where I'd left him, lashed face-down over the back the mare plow-horse he'd rode out into the Kentucky hills to ambush me. Or at least, to ambush the first clockwork man he'd seen with anything worth stealing. Just my bad luck, and his, that it had been me.

"We're going to find you a gearsmith, you damned fool. Now, you'd be best to shut your horn, Rusty Jack. That rifle-ball in your chest shifts half-and-inch and binds on your mainspring or blocks your escapement, that will be the end of you!"

"What do you care, Liberty? It was you what put that ball in me in the first place! You want me propped up again so you can take another shot at killing me? You just mad you missed?"

I cursed my luck in that my shot had taken every power of movement and action from Jack, except the ability to speak. He had hardly stopped talking since the moment we'd met, before and after I'd shot him. "I don't miss, Jack. *Never.* I was built a Confederate Artilleryman, and thanks to the special gears and forks in my poor, cracked, head, shooting comes as natural for me as larceny seems to come for you. I hit you right where I was aiming for you. But I'm not a gearsmith, so I had to guess where I could shoot to stop you without killing you. It could have been a worse guess."

"It could have been better, Brass!"

"Jack, if you're trying to rile me into finishing you off, you're doing a good job of it!"

I had no plan to do that, of course. I'd seen plenty of killing in my short days; of men of metal, and men of flesh. War had left its scars on my metal shell, and the works far beneath.

No, there would be no killing him, if I could chose in the matter. I just hoped to end his prattling, dump him in some town where they could deal with him, and ride on in peace. I was going nowhere, and I was in a hurry to get there.

"Jack, I'll number it among my best days when I can get your rusty hide fixed up enough to turn over to the nearest lawman!"

"I can't see nothing, hanging this way! Where you taking me? Dryhill? Thousandsticks?"

"I have no idea," I said truthfully. "First town I find headed west. But I've never been this way before, and I hope never to come this way again."

"You mean you're wandering blind? You don't want to do that, Liberty Brass! There are dangers in these Kentucky hills! Turn me over so I can see, and I'll guide you right to the nearest good town!"

"Or into some lair full of your bandit friends? No thank-you, Jack. I'll just go on as I am until I find someone whose directions I can trust, or until I see the smoke from some settlement."

"Please, Liberty! My camp is half-a-day's ride southeast of where you shot me, and though I haunt that trail you was riding from time to time, me and mine don't go into the hills west of there."

"You never been this way, what are you afeared of, Jack? A lawman who looks unfairly on clockwork bandits?"

"Just afeared of stories, Liberty, but stories I've heard again and again. Tales of clockwork men come into these hills and never return."

"And if all goes well, Jack, I'll be another such, as I just keep riding on. And you as well, as you face some justice for your deeds."

But truth was, I felt my gears twinge with concern as I rode on into that fog, following a narrow trail across land that tilted up at crazy angles, land with no top or bottom, all edges or horizons lost in the mist, trees making black and threatening shadows in the gloom. I had been riding blindly for so long, I'd forgotten to concern myself with such dangers as might lay ahead. I had begun my travels running from war, but the shots and screams of Gettysburg were far behind me now. Perhaps it was time started finding something to ride *to*, and not just something to ride away from.

I was considering how much of Rusty Jack's direction I

might be able to trust, when I felt Piston's normally confident gait beneath me falter, and heard the fine gears that drove his ears buzz, the delicately curved metal horns turning this way and that, seeking some distant sound. It was the same thing that had warned me of Jack, in his hidden sniper's perch in the fork of an old oak tree.

I swiveled my head, seeking the source of my horse's uneasiness, when the sound of a cocking carbine came to my own ears.

"Stop where you are, stranger, and show your empty hands, high and wide!"

The voice came from behind some bushes up ahead and to the right of the trail.

"See?" Jack yelled. "I tried to warn you!"

"Shut up!" I cried. But at least these didn't seem to be Jack's bandit friends, come to rescue him, or seek revenge for his shooting.

I looked at where my own rifle hung ahead of my saddle, and considered trying to get off a shot, but I couldn't see my adversary. Being a clockwork man who never misses doesn't help when you can't see what to shoot. I also heard another sound behind me and up the hill, the snorting of a large animal. It was just as likely a second gun was trained on me from behind. No, perhaps my chance for action would come later.

A large horse, a plow-horse like Jack's, since even a the lightest clockwork man is a heavy burden for a flesh-horse, walked out from behind the bushes. It's rider was a small and slender clockwork man of dark hammered tin and copper turned pale green, like moss. He wore nothing but a green wool vest, a bowler hat, and a gun-belt around his middle.

I watched the barrel of "copper-back's" carbine as he rode cautiously closer.

Just as my artilleryman's works let me shoot without missing, I could figure from second-to-second just where his gun was aimed. His hands were quick and true, but his flesh mount constantly threw off his shot, and it took time for his sights to lock back on my main-spring. There were any number of times when his shot would have gone wild, and I could have taken him, but not without possibly getting shot in the back by his hidden friend, so I let him do as he would. They looked serious, but something about them made me question their certainty of intent. Unlike old Jack behind me, they seemed more cautious than vicious.

Copper-back rode up and took my rifle. He checked my person and saddle-bags for handguns, and finding none, instructed me to lower my arms and place my hands behind me. He produced a piece of steel wire, and bound my wrists together.

He then turned his attention to Jack, riding back, and prodding at him with the muzzle of his gun. As he poked at Jack's head, it turned a bit so that Jack could see what was going on.

"Is he dead?" Asked copper-back.

"Careful there! I ain't dead, demon! Just up an paralyzed is what I am! If you aim to kill me, make it quick!"

"Quiet, Jack," I said. "Don't be giving anyone ideas."

Copper-back looked up the hill. "Come on down, Kettle! They won't be going us no harm!"

A large shape appeared out of the fog, a bulky automaton riding on an even larger ox. I had never seen the likes of him before. He was dark, with a rounded body, heavy limbs and wide head. He was built like a steam-man, all blackened cast iron and steel, greasy where he was oiled, and rusty where he wasn't. But he was no steam man, and a bit of his heavy mainspring could be seen through a mica window in his chest.

Kettle looked me over. "That's some fine horse you've got, stranger." His voice was deep and scratchy. "Looks strong enough to carry even my weight."

"Don't get any ideas," I said. "Piston has a mind of his own, and he won't ride for none but me. You think he's strong, you might just see how far he can buck your iron carcass."

Kettle laughed a scratchy laugh, like a cog-wheel in need of oil. "He has a twist in his spring, this one. Keep an eye on him, Copperpot."

So, the smaller one had a name. "Copperpot," I said, trying it on.

"That's *Captain* Copperpot to you," he said. "Captain of the Steam Man's guard, and he'll be wanting to see you two, and this clockwork horse of yours too."

"Does this steam man have a name?"

"He's just the Steam Man," said Copperpot. "What other name would he need? How many steam men do you know?"

And in truth, I had never met one, only heard and read stories of them. Steam men were the first mechanical men, like ancient heroes or gods to us clockwork men. While most clockwork men came from factories, where we were made in mass, like rifles or cannon or – cookpots, each steam-man was unique. Each a product of, and symbol of, the genius, ego, and avarice of Man. They were legendary, for their powers, their volatile natures, their great virtues -- and their great vices. And though they were powerful, few had ever been built, and most had burned brightly rather than living long.

Part of me thrilled that I might finally meet such a legendary steam man. And part of me quaked at the prospect.

We rode till the sun stood high in the sky, burning off the fog and giving way to broken clouds tinged with gray. And finally we came to signs of habitation, passing fences of stone and split wood, and up a well-packed road marked with the regular passage of wagons, till we rounded a bend, and the house came into view.

Somehow it seemed right that a steam man should have a castle. Well, it was short of a castle, but it was a big house, like the plantation houses I had seen in the South. And once, at least, it had been grand. It had two floors, with a domed cupola on the slate roof. A great porch ran the length of the front of the house, held up by six Greek columns.

But it showed signs of age and neglect. Broken tiles hung from the roof, there were broken and missing panes among the hundreds in the upper floor, and the white paint was cracked and peeling, revealing bare stone and graying wood beneath. That paint not gone, was often streaked with moldy green and black.

But everywhere, there were also signs of industrious activity, and ongoing repair. Clockwork men of every shape and size, many of them freed Confederates like myself, chipped at peeling paint, hammered at loose boards, or chopped away at overgrown rose-bushes. Though the rest of the house looked rough, the front stairs were clean and in good repair, and the brass fittings on the front-door were polished until they gleamed like gold.

We stopped in front of the stairs, and Kettle unhitched the lead to Jack's horse from Piston and lead him off to one side. "Ho!" I said. "Where are you taking him? He's got a rifle ball loose in his chest! He needs a gearsmith!"

"We've got a machine repair shop back by the mine. They'll look him over there and see what they can do with him." Copperpot and Kettle exchanged a glance, but I didn't know what it meant.

"Don't let them take me, Liberty! This place is the devil's own work! Mark my words!"

But my hands were still tightly bound. "Sorry, Jack. There's nothing I can do about it. It was your own sorry doings that brought you to this place." I watched as Jack and his horse were lead away around a path up the back of the house by Kettle, still mounted on his big, grey, ox. As I saw him, hanging there limp and even more helpless than I, I couldn't help but to feel sorry for him. I yelled, "Try to shut your horn for once, Jack, and maybe they'll have mercy and fix you up." But that weak bit of advice and comfort was all I had to offer him.

Copperpot had, by this time, climbed down from his horse and was walking up to me, still carrying his carbine, still aiming it at me more or less. Again, I might have taken him, but my hands were still bound, and I'd seen at least a dozen clockwork men since reaching the Steam Man's plantation, with an unknown number beyond at the shop and mine mentioned, and Maker knows how many more elsewhere.

Besides, I still had not seen the steam man, and curiosity is its own kind of devilment.

With some difficulty, I was able to swing my right leg over the saddle, and as I did, I was amazed to see that Piston was standing on three legs, his left front leg curled back, his hoof flat towards the sky to serve as a step. Would the wonders of this horse never cease?

If Copperpot noticed, he didn't let on. He just watched me impatiently, then urged me up the steps with the end of his gun. The door swung open before I could reach it, and standing there, straight and true, was the first clockwork butler I had ever laid eyes on. He was fully dressed in a fine suit, as a flesh-butler would have been, and even his feet were shod in polished, black, leather. His head and body, what I could see of it, were made of polished brass, but there were decorative silver figurative pieces on his head and the backs of his hands.

The butler took but a moment's glance down at my bindings before recovering his full composure. "I'll take your hat, sir." He took the battered cavalry officer's hat that I used to keep the rain out of my head, and collected Copperpot's bowler as well.

To our right, a large, arched doorway lead into a larger room, and through it boomed a voice such as I had never heard before, composed as it was of the sound of horns, pipes, and whistles, melded with angelic grace into one booming note of power: "Copperpot! Have you gone mad! Set this man free at once!"

Copperpot seemed to lose interest in me entirely. He shuffled over in front of the doorway and stood submissively before the hidden speaker within, his carbine clutched crossways in front his knees, his hands twisting as though he was trying to wring it out like a wet rag. "But boss, I found him out around the southeast creek trail with that half-dead clockwork man hanging from the horse behind him! Who knows what mischief he's up to?"

"Have you got lenses in your head, Copperpot, or did you switch them out for coal to keep your head warm? This is no ordinary clockwork man! This is an *artilleryman*, the finest clockwork the Confederates ever managed to turn out! An officer and gentleman among metal men! Release him at once, and bring him to my company!"

Copperpot bowed his head and backed away. "Yes, Boss! At once!"

He rushed over and began to untwist the wire from my wrists. But as he did, he leaned close to my ear-horn and said in a whisper, "don't you get any ideas about bringing any harm to the Steam Man. You may not see me, but me and my carbine won't be far away!"

And with that, he pulled the wire loose, and stepped back, disappearing down a hallway towards the back of the house.

The butler gestured, and I cautiously stepped forward and peered around the corner.

While other rooms of the house that I could see through open doors were largely bare and undecorated, this one was elaborately furnished with elaborate rugs, fine draperies, and elaborately carved and upholstered furniture. The walls were covered with landscape paintings, large mirrors with gilt frames, and silver sconces. And finally, the source of all my expectations and anxieties came into view.

The Steam Man sat in a vast, wing-backed chair, before a cold and empty fireplace, shoving coal into his glowing red chest. Sensing my hesitation, he waved me in, before swinging shut his firebox door, hiding the glow but for a small, round, sight-hole in the middle. Smoke belched up from the smokestack sprouting up from his back and rolled out across the ceiling, already well stained with soot. That it was not yet black could only be accounted by constant cleaning on someone's part. The smoke pooled there, until it was sucked by a draft out the open upper light of a window in a far corner.

The steam man was large; broad of body and limb, and his round, glass eyes glowed soft orange from some hidden source of heat. He had a nose like an iron carrot that served no purpose other than decorative that I could see, and a heavy jaw and mouth that opened like a shutter to reveal his speaking horns and pipes. The top of his head was crowned with a tall iron hat that seemed to be permanently attached to his skull, though it seemed to be functional as well as decorative, as the top of it would occasionally vent a cascade of billowing steam.

I could see that his chair had been modified to support his great weight, the original legs having been replaced by a massive pedestal of solid hardwood. Next to him was a small table, on which rested an oil-can, an open book, and a square wooden checker board, but set with taller ivory pieces that I recognized as the game of chess. He seemed to make some use of the chair's original arms, but he could hardly be using the back at all, since the heat of his smokestack would have likely caused the upholstery to burst into flame.

"As you can see," said the Steam Man, noticing the direction of my lenses, "there is much work to do here on the estate, on the house and otherwise. I mean to have myself a proper chair made of metal, strong and fireproof, with a hood like a forge and a chimney to take away my smoke. It has been in my mind for some time, but resources are so limited, and there is always so much to do!"

Seeing my hesitation, the Steam Man urged me closer with a graceful sweep of his massive arm. "Please, artilleryman, come closer and accept my hospitality and deepest apologies. Copperpot and Kettle mean well, but they're not the brightest of mechanical souls. Between the two of them they could hardly put together enough head-gears to drive a good pocket-watch!"

The Steam Man stood at my approach, the chair groaning as it was relieved of his weight, and the floor creaking at having taken over this great burden. "You may simply call me the Steam Man, good-sir. And may I be so bold as to ask you to share your own?"

"Liberty Brass," I said.

"That is surely not your military designation?"

"I had one in the past, but I do not use it any more. The name Liberty was given to me by a confederate flesh men whom I served, in reference to the famous cracked bell of Phil-adelphia. I took a liking to it, and when I took the freedom offered by President Lincoln in his second proclamation, I made the name my own."

"An excellent name, and an excellent story to go with it! Come! Sit with me and enjoy the simple comforts of my adopted home!" He gestured towards a sturdy but more conventional padded chair a few feet from his own.

I carefully perched myself on the edge of the seat. It creaked a bit, but held solid under my weight. It was a strange and largely unfamiliar sensation. A clockwork man in good working order is as comfortable leaning against a wall as they are sitting in a chair, and on those occasions I have done it, it was usually for the mental comfort of flesh-men who were also sitting and wished not to have me towering over them.

"May I offer you any comfort? A winding perhaps? We have several fine winder-men here at the plantation, and the finest steam-winder-mill you have ever seen, powered of course, by the excellent Kentucky coal that we mine here on the premises!"

Suddenly, the existence of this place made a great deal more sense. It is rare to see so many clockwork men together without the presence of people, simply because they must be wound. There are of course winder-men, who must in turn be wound by winder-mills. I have seen such mills powered by wind, by water, and even by the industry of animals such as oxen, horse, or mule, but it would take a great engine indeed to keep so many men wound at once.

"My spring is military grade, and good for several more days," I answered, "but I would be most appreciative if someone could wind my clockwork horse, Piston, out front."

The Steam Man nodded. "I saw him as you rode up. A fine and amazing animal! I wish but that we could have a dozen like him here at the plantation. It is a burden providing food and pasture for those flesh-animals that we do use here."

"I have seen a few other clockwork horses and mules," I said, "but Piston is one-of-a-kind so far as I know. Strong, intelligent, and *willful*. I did not deceive your men when I claimed he would ride for nobody but me. Since he was given to me by a dying winder-man, has attached himself to me like a pet, and he complains in his own way at the lack of company."

"Fantastic!" The Steam Man clapped his hands in delight,

and it sounded like two blacksmith's hammers slung together. "You are a great source of wonder and amusement to me, Liberty Brass! A great refreshment to me, for as I have tried to create my little society of mechanical men here in this place, I have come to hunger for the company of intelligent and refined fellows worthy of my time. I have assembled a goodly number of clockwork men here at the plantation, but they are mostly simple laborers, rough company of poor manufacture."

"You might be disappointed then," I said. "I was made simply to be a soldier, built for no more refinements than a tent or an ammo cart can offer, and I have traveled even rougher since I have been on my own, keeping bad company on those rare occasional when I have kept any at all."

"You do yourself a disservice," he said. "Quality of build will tell. One does not aim an iron ball across a battlefield or field-repair a cannon without intelligence and refinement far beyond the average clockwork man. And," his eyes swiveled towards the crack in the brass casing of my head, "doubtless you have seen hard times. But you are obviously a victim of your circumstances."

As I was. That cannonball that had grazed my skull had done more than leave a crack down my face, it had also damaged the governor that all wind-up men possess, that mechanism that makes it impossible for us to directly harm a human being. Though I had aimed and loaded many a cannon in wartime, I had never fired one. A human officer had always pulled the cord, a fact that offers me no comfort at all. But I had greater guilts, and more blood on my hands than I cared to remember, much less tell. I was, and am, a retched creature, seeking in vain to compensate for the crime of my own existence.

"We have mechanical resources here, my friend. Perhaps," he said, "there is something that we can do to repair you, to remove those scars on your fine mechanism!

"I think there is no repairing..." I did not finish the sentence, for a most important and wonderful thought hummed itself in existence inside my broken head. If I were to remain in this place, a society of only automatons, then my moral handicap would be of no consequence at all! If there were no humans to harm, then my lack of internal governance would have no meaning, and I could bring harm to no other being of flesh! It would not undo what I had already done, but it would eliminate the possibility of further downfall.

And thus, I fell silent on the matter, and remained so the rest of the afternoon, grateful for the possibility, yet fearful to discuss it least I be cast out of this new paradise.

The Steam Man's appetite for conversation seemed limitless. He demanded to know every detail of my journey from the battlefields of Virginia to the hills of Kentucky, and every adventure along the way. He also seemed fascinated with my experiences serving as a Confederate artilleryman, and despite my reluctance, drew out tales of battle and war. Though I tried to keep myself to those tales of honor, courage, and selflessness that were the all-too rare fruit of warfare, he seemed to prefer those tales of cruelty, injustice, and the horrors that flesh-men visit on one another.

I pondered this as the butler, whom I had learned was called "Gears," came into the room and lit a series of oil lamps to hold back the falling darkness outside.

"Perhaps, my friend," said the Steam Man, "you waste too much concern for the carnage of war. Perhaps it would be better if flesh-men, with all their failings, simply wiped each other from the face of the Earth, making way for us automatons. For lacking those weaknesses of flesh, we are clearly their superiors and rightful successors."

And though this seemed the most theoretical discussions, it made me uneasy. It was my goal to hold ill-will to no creature merely by the fact of their existence. I had seen humanity at its worst, but I had also seen Rusty Jack and his like many times, and knew that men of metal were as vulnerable to failings of spirit as men of flesh.

But that was soon forgotten as our conversation drifted to other topics, and ran far into the evening. Finally, the Steam Man stood. "I fear I must be about the business of may plantation. My butler will show you to quarters where you may spend the evening."

I was puzzled. "Surely you can't work in such darkness."

He laughed; a deep whistling wheeze. "It is the curse of Clockwork men that, though they cannot truly sleep, they see poorly in the darkness, and thus are prisoners of the night. Like you, I have no need for sleep, but I have no such limitations. My eyes see by heat as well as light, and the heat of my own furnace illuminates my way like a spotlight. I find this time ideal to inspect certain of my holdings and the progress of the day's work."

I pondered this curious fact as Gears, the butler, carrying a lamp to light our way, lead me up a grand stair and down a hall to a bedroom. By his lamp, I saw the furniture to be dusty, and the bed-frame empty of mattress, bedding, or even slats. But I had no need of such human finery, and it concerned me not at all. I was more bothered by the click of the lock as the butler departed.

With some difficulty in the darkness, I found the knob and

discovered that it indeed resisted turning. But where would I go in such darkness anyway? I felt my way to a corner, locked my leg joints, and leaned against the wall.

Now, while clockwork men have no need of sleep, it would be wasteful to expend the full energy of our springs through the night, and so we have a setting where we become our own alarm clocks, our escapements set to a slow speed, barely enough to keep our minds humming and maintain a slight awareness to light and sound so that we may be awakened by morning or any trouble before then.

I placed myself in this state of rest and the black hours melted by. Though we do not dream, during the night my slow thoughts turn to fancy, and I imagined a peaceful and grand utopia of mechanical men, not a plantation, but an entire city, perhaps an entire country, with the Steam Man as its beloved king.

I was disturbed from my musings by the morning light shining through the shutters, and a pounding at the bedroom door. "Brass," yelled Copperpots angry voice, "get yourself downstairs and deal with this cursed horse of yours. We've not been able to move him all night. He still stands in front of the big house, more stubborn than any mule, and refuses to leave sight of the front-door. Rain threatens, and he won't move his sorry self to the barn!"

I would have smiled, if I had been equipped with lips. My faithful steed had of course refused to move without my instruction. I went to the door and found it unlocked. I went down stairs, out the front door, and found Copperpot and Kettle standing at the foot of the porch steps.

"There he is," said Copperpot.

Piston stood only a few yards from where I'd left him,

having moved closer to the door. From his tracks in the mud, he'd circled in front of the door many times, and had all but walked onto the porch. I took his reigns. "Come on, boy," I tugged him in the direction Copperpot was pointing, presumably to the stable.

Much to my surprise, he resisted, something I could not remember him doing before. "Come on, Piston! Rain's a coming!"

He just stared at me with his glass eyes, glancing occasionally at the door, and at Copperpot and Kettle. Then he turned, and tried to pull me away from the house, back in the direction we had come in.

"Piston! What's got into you! Get back here!"

I yanked at his reigns with all my might, and though even that would not have been enough to stay my steed were he truly determined, he reluctantly turned and followed my lead. We walked around the back of the house and along a split-rail fence toward a white-washed carriage house. I hillside rose up steeply behind the house, and though much of it was covered with trees, I could see a tall wooden derrick rising above the treetops, several buildings, large and small, and somewhat nearer the house, a large brick building with a chimney that belched black smoke.

I nodded towards it. "That's the mine then?"

Copperpot seemed annoyed that I'd even try to talk to him. Finally he said, "It is, and the winder-mill."

"Where's the shop you took Rusty Jack? I'd like to check up on him."

Copperpot and Kettle looked at each other for a moment before Copperpot answered. "It's a ways up there, and the mine is a dangerous place for them not familiar with it. You let us take care of that outlaw of your'n."

Kettle made a scratchy sound that might have been a laugh, and I felt that I had missed the joke.

When we returned to the house, the Steam Man was not to be found, and Gears, the butler, directed me to wait in the library. As with most of the house, the furnishings were damaged and haphazard, but I was more interested in the books. Though some seemed damaged by water or fire, there was a considerable collection, and being constructed to read, I had no trouble passing the rest of the morning perusing works of science and literature.

In particular I was taken with a work describing tales of Greek myth, and the capricious meddling of Gods with mortal men. I was entranced in its pages when the butler reappeared. "The master has returned to the house," he announced, "and will receive your company in the parlor."

The Steam Man was back in his familiar chair, puffs of smoke from his stack spreading across the blackened ceiling, even as a trio of clockwork men unknown to me frantically tried to direct them out the open windows using large, paper, fans.

Gears vanished for a moment, only to return with an oil can on a silver tray. He sat the tray on a side table, and began to oil the Steam Man's many joints, an operation to which the Steam Man paid about as much attention to as a flower might the attendance of a bee.

The Steam Man again tried to extract from me tales of my past, but I was more interested at that moment about my future.

"I have been considering my prospects. My intentions for

myself since parting the Confederate Army have been at best vague, though it has been my general intention to journey west to the spaces of the frontier, where I might be spared the company of men, and the troubles that go with them. But now that I have seen this place, I now recognize the possibility of such isolation may be nearer at hand than I imagined. I would like to stay, if you would have me."

The Steam Man clapped his great hands together with a clank. "Excellent! I had been hoping you might desire to remain here! Though we have many mechanical men here, few if any can match your qualities and capabilities -- present company excepted, of course!" He laughed.

He studied my manner for a moment, curiously. "I sense that something still troubles you, my friend Liberty. What can it be?"

I looked around, at Gears with his oil can, at the clockwork men fanning away the smoke, and others toiling in the grounds outside, setting fences, clearing brush, and repairing the house. "I see around me all manner of great industry in service of this place, yet I sit here doing nothing."

"You are hardly doing nothing, Liberty! I have not had such interesting conversation since I held audience with the great princes of India and the crowns of Europe!"

I brushed my hand through the air, as a flesh-man might brush away a fly. "I could never be content serving merely as an entertainment," I said. "Not only would I feel it an inadequate contribution to the fold, but I was built as a military man, for action, not for languor. Books and conversation are fine to a point, but beyond that I need useful activity or my gears will certainly begin to thrash."

"But of course, and I have considered this point, how your

skills and abilities might be useful to us here. We have no need of an artilleryman at present, though I can imagine circumstances under which that might change one day. But I have been lead to believe you have other, related, skills. For instance, I have heard you are quite handy with a hand-held gun as well as a cannon. In fact, I have heard that you never miss."

"You heard this from Copperpot?"

"I heard it from the clockwork man you shot, Rusty Jack. I made it a point to interview him last night."

"And he told you that?"

"He was most talkative, when properly approached. But it was clear he was not a man to be trusted, so I seek verification of this most outrageous statement."

I answered with unusual candor. "That is a notion that I have never discouraged. It is true, my hand is swift and true, my eyes sharp, and my mind built for the instantaneous calculation of trajectories and ballistics. But I am subject, as any shooter, to the vagaries of wind and the imperfect manufacture of firearms and shells."

"Then," he said, "you *have* missed."

I corrected him. "No sir. I have not missed -- *yet.*"

He laughed heartily, the deep notes of his whistles rattling the rippled panes in the windows. "Then there must certainly be a place for you in my guard!" He looked around and lowered his voice. "Perhaps even as captain, once you have proved yourself worthy of my trust. To be honest, Copperpot was always a reluctant choice on my part, and Kettle is a idiot, unworthy of even consideration."

Having finished his task, the butler placed the oil can back on his tray and lifted it. "Will there be anything else, sir?"

"That will be all for now, Gears."

I watched him walk away, and observed the men still busy with their fans. As I had sometimes noticed with flesh-men of status, servants were all but invisible to them, and this seemed true of the Steam Man as well.

I realized that one word the Steam Man had spoken stuck in my head-gears like a piece of grit; "trust."

"It is hard," I said, "to be an effective member of the guard, or to be the man who cannot miss, if I do not have a firearm to fire. Am I to construe from this lack that there is still an issue of trust in my loyalty?"

The Steam Man made a guttural noise, like a man clearing his throat. "Our enterprise here is still young, and still fragile, Liberty. As you know better than anyone, not all mechanical men share the same nature. Not all can be trusted to place our greater cause above petty interests and other loyalties. I worry that men, as they hear of our community, may fear it, and seek to destroy it. I worry that even now, they might attempt to send spies into our midst."

"I am no spy," I said, "and I serve none but myself."

The Steam Man nodded. "And that is my belief, Liberty Brass. But I have learned in my years that patience and caution are free to those that will have them. There will be time for you to gain my trust, and time for me to use your skills. You must be patient as well."

Must, I wondered, I be cautious also?

Gears returned. "Sir, the mechanic has arrived from the shops. I have sent him to wait on the back porch."

The Steam Man stood. "Excellent! See, my friend? Already your patience is rewarded. I have summoned my best man to look at the damage to your poor skull and to see what may be done about it."

"Very little I fear. The parts are too delicate, and cannot be repaired without stopping my works."

"Let an expert be the judge of that! Perhaps, at least, that crack in your head can be repaired so as to restore your handsome visage! Now, follow Gears. He will take you."

I was lead through to the back of the house and through the unused kitchen, its stoves cold and rusty, and out onto a broad back porch that, from its furnishings, had once served as a laundry and an extension of the kitchen in good weather. A table had been set up in the middle of the porch, upon which an oilcloth wrap had been set out, into which many pockets had been sewn, all of which were filled with a wide array of gear-smith's tools.

To my surprise, standing behind the table sorting through the tools, was a tall, dark-skinned flesh-man, what they call a 'negro.' He wore coveralls over a white shirt with the sleeves rolled up to the elbow. A few smudges of grease and oil marred the shirt, though it looked recently laundered. As he shifted his footing, I heard a clanking sound and looked down. As I did, something moved behind the table, and I stepped back, thinking there might be some animal there.

Instead, there was a clockwork man. Or what was left of one, anyways. He was a type I recognized from my military days as a courier, small, light, and swift of foot. Or this one would have been, if he had feet. Or legs.

I took another step back. The little man looked up at me with green-tinted eye lenses, and I could see him shuffling along the floor on his hands. His body ended cleanly at the waist, and there appeared to have been some work done to seal up the truncation, something like an iron cup covering the end of his waist joint, and providing a smooth surface that could slide along the ground as he moved.

I could also see one other thing: the stout length of iron chain that connected from a ring on his back to a cuff locked around the flesh-man's ankle.

"No need to be afraid of my little friend here," said the flesh man. "He is the most harmless thing you will meet today, certainly."

The little automaton nodded at me in greeting, but did not speak, and I wondered if he could.

"My name is Joshua, said the mechanic. His name," he pointed at the mechanical man by his feet, "is Deadweight, and it is a cruel reference to his function. As you can see, he was damaged in the great war, and brought to this place by a companion -- since departed. It was the judgment of the Steam Man that he was not good for much but slowing others down, and so he was assigned as my caretaker." He reached down and placed has hand on top of Deadweight's head. "But in truth, I have become quite fond of him, and though I would gratefully lose the chain that connects us, I would miss him if we were ever parted."

"You are a slave," I said slowly, unsure if I meant is as a statement of fact, or a question."

He nodded. "I am."

"How did this come to be?"

He looked down to his tools and smiled sadly. "I was born to slavery, and though there have been false hopes, I fear I shall die a slave too. How I came to this place is a long story, perhaps for another time, but in most respects I am treated better here than by my former master. I am given good clothing, books to read, a comfortable bed. The food is bad, for I must cook for myself, and I am no cook, but I am always given plenty of supplies, and occasionally even spirits or wine. I enjoy my work when I can repair or maintain machines such as yourself. There are other duties that I--" His face tightened, and grimaced as though in pain. "I have been in worse places, I suppose." There a heavy wooden stool next to the table. He gestured at it. "Sit here, so I can examine you."

I sat, and the wood creaked under my weight, but held.

The man picked up a large magnifying lens and leaned close to my face. He peered at the crack in my skull. "Hmmm," he said.

He shifted the lens to a different perspective. "Hmmm."

I wondered what he was seeing, but I was hesitant to ask. I started to turn toward him, but he pushed his hand against the side of my head firmly. "Stay still, please."

The man changed position again, and I heard the *clank-tump-shuffle-thump* as Deadweight moved with him.

"Deadweight does not speak?"

Joshua did not look up from his task as he answered. "He can. There is no mechanical fault the prevents him, but he rarely does. I fear his mind may have been damaged in the war as well as his body. Perhaps this is why the Steam Man has never allowed me to even try to replace his legs."

"Where," I mused, "would you even find parts in such a place?"

Again, the man's face tightened. "There are ways," he said, clearly uncomfortable with the matter.

I tried to change the subject. "How did you become a gearsmith?"

He laughed. "Me? A gearsmith? I am nothing of the sort. But I have always been interested in machines and tools, and though the Steam Man is reluctant to depend on any human, there are aspects of automaton repair that mechanical man seem ill-equipped, perhaps by design, to grasp." He reached down and picked up a small, pointed hook and began to scrape around the crack in my head. "In truth, I know my own skills are limited, and from my readings, there are aspects of mechanical men's making that exceed even the most skilled and learned of men. The first harmonic thought engine was created quite by accident, and no man knows exactly how it works." He scratched at my head some more, moved his glass back and forth in front of his eye, and stepped back. "Hmmm."

I had been skeptical about this from the start. "I expect there is nothing you can do?"

"I doubt the best gearsmith in the world would dare to touch what is wrong with your head. A shard of metal has pushed in the side the governing chamber on your resonator. It is a wonder that your brain did not simply cease to function. But if it is something of a miracle that you can think at all, then perhaps it is no more surprising miracle that you continue to do so." He scratched his head and put down his glass on the table. "You suffer not at all from this injury?"

"There is a matter," I said with some reluctance. "As all clockwork men are made to prohibit the killing or harm of flesh men... Since my injury, I enjoy no such prohibition."

He furrowed his brow. "Oh." The full implication then

seemed to strike him, and he stepped back so quickly that Deadweight could not follow, and the chain pulled tight. *"Oh!"*

"I mean you no harm," I said. "You can kill a man as easily as I, but I trust you would not do so without just cause or provocation, and perhaps even then."

He seemed to relax a little. "Like ourselves and steam men, you suffer the curse, of Adam, then," he said, "the knowledge, and therefore the possibility, of good and evil."

"I had never considered it against that human story, but yes, I suppose it is so. Though I have no Eve on which to pass blame, and I had a cannon-ball for my apple."

And despite himself, Joshua laughed. "That you did, friend!"

"Think not that, despite my injury and its resulting failings, that I am without care or sympathy. For example, it troubles me greatly that you are a slave, and if it is possible, more profoundly because you are the slave of a mechanical man. One I have considered calling friend."

Joshua seemed as though he wanted to say something, his lips pressed hard together, one eye twitching slightly.

A tinny, scattered voice echoed from below him, as though from the end of a long pipe. "Choose your friends carefully."

Joshua glared down at the little automaton. "Hush, Deadweight! You'll get us in trouble!"

It was in that moment of that my gun-hand shot out like lightning and took a small pen knife that I had seen among the tools. I hit it beneath my palm, and when there was a chance, tucked it into the back of my belt. It was time I saw more of the Steam Man's plantation, and for that, I would need my freedom at night.

That night, as the butler lead me to my room, I took with me a book from the library, and used it as an excuse to request a lamp be left in my room. In fact, I did read for a while, but with the lamp turned as low as possible to conserve the oil. I waited until, though my window, I saw the Steam Man depart on his rounds and the house became quiet.

It was only then I removed the knife from its hiding place. It was a small folding knife with a flat blade and a well-worn ivory handle. I brought out the blade and using the lamp examined the door frame. The wood was dry and had shrunk, creating a slight void between the door jam and the frame. I was able to slip the knife blade far enough to bow the jam out yet farther, and slide the tip of the blade to reach and depress the latch. With a bit of fumbling, the door came open with a slight click.

I opened the door only a crack. The hallway appeared nearly dark, except for a little moonlight coming through a window at the end. I listened carefully for several minutes, but I heard no movement in the house. With great care, I picked up the lamp made my exit. The key had been left in the lock, so I had no difficulty locking the bedroom door behind me.

When not specifically needed by the Steam Man, Gears spent most of his time in a small Butler's pantry off the hall behind the parlor, and I suspected that was where he spent his nights as well. I resolved to stay as far clear of these areas as possible. Earlier, when passing through the kitchen, I had seen the bottom of a servant's stair, along the back wall, and had little difficulty in finding the top of it. I followed it down, went out the back door and off the porch, heading in the direction of the mine.

I stopped briefly at the carriage-house to check on Piston. Upon recognizing me, he became agitated, kicking at his stall, and making vocal his unease with our current situation, an uneasiness I now shared. But I feared he would draw the attention of someone in the house, and did my best to calm him. "There, there, my friend. You may get your wish that we leave this place soon, but there are things I have to know before I leave, and I've got to learn what happened to Rusty Jack."

Seeming to understand me, Piston snorted at the mention of Jack's name.

"He's a pole-cat, for sure, but we brought him here, and I feel some responsibility for him. Now you just wait here, and with luck, we might be clear of here by dawn."

But he still great agitated as I moved to depart, and so I left the gate to his stall unhooked. This seemed to ease his tension some, and it mattered little, since I knew he could have kicked it off its hinges at any time. Only my words could truly bind him to this spot. "Wait here!"

I left the carriage-house and followed a well worn path toward where I believed the mine to be. To my surprise, even at that late hour, I soon could hear the sounds of the mine, and see lights from the buildings there. I supposed that, in the deep darkness of a mine, there was no night and day, and therefore no reason to schedule operations by the strictures of the sun.

The first building I passed was the winder-mill, small in comparison to the structures beyond it. I could see the outline of a stone smokestack jutting from its roof into the night sky, and the flickering of the firebox on the boiler within. Every few minutes, a heavy-set winder-man would arrive, and at the same interval, one would leave, his great spring fully wound, to head back to the mine, presumably to rewind the workers there.

I steered well clear of the mine-head, a tower made of stout timbers that supported the steam hoist that raised coal from the mine shaft, and sent miners into its depths. I had little trouble keeping myself hidden, as everywhere were great piles of coal, black artificial mountains nearly invisible, except in outline, even when I shined my lamp onto them. In coming around one of these piles, a happened upon a tool shed with a lantern hanging next to its locked door. I traded my lamp for the more portable and durable lantern, and made my way further into the canyons between the black mountains.

I spotted another shed with light showing through its windows, and peered through one cautiously from an angle. Inside, a heavy, wooden bench sat against the far wall, and an array of tools hung on pegs behind it. On the bench was the partly disassembled arm of a winder man, recognizable by its heavy construction, and the substantial gearing that drove the rotating winder-hand. This then had to be the shop where Rusty Jack had been taken.

I moved closer, and indeed, I saw the edge-part of what looked like Jack, sitting on a box, his back against the wall. I moved closer still, and saw the whole of them, or what was left. His right arm was missing, his chest opened, his mainspring removed, and his head nowhere to be seen.

In horror, I leapt for the door, dashing inside to see what had befallen him. And there, unseen until now, I found Joshua standing at a smaller bench, the parts of Jack's head spread out across the table in front of him like a disassembled clock.

Joshua stared at me, eyes wide with surprise, his mouth

hanging open and silent. Finally, he looked down at Jack's disassembled head and the tool in his hand, as though he had suddenly found himself covered in blood. "I should have told you," he said. "I should have found the same courage to speak as Deadweight, and warned you away from this place. I should have, but I feared too much for my own, worthless, hide!"

I might have condemned him then, and filled myself with hate, and lashed out at him as I once had another flesh man. But I only trembled, my poor gears struggling to understand what I was seeing. On shelves and hooks behind him hung assorted parts from at least a dozen mechanical men, arms, legs, gears, cams, torsos and heads. To one side, an entire bucked was filled with eye lenses, glittering and blind. I was willing to wager Jack had not been the last to meet their end in this shed.

"Did you kill him?" I asked.

"Though I do not expect you to believe me, I swear I did not. Copperpot and Kettle held him while the Steam Man picked at his works, holding back his mainspring to the edge of death, and then releasing it, again and again until all the Steam Man's questions were answered. And he was still alive when the Steam Man took lose his head and left me the rest to salvage for parts, so that in his death, I might at least strive to save the lives of others."

I remembered the Steam Man's admission that he had questioned Jack, and the dark hints now apparent in his words. "I have some cause to believe your story," I said, "of the other's guilt, even if I lack absolute evidence of your own innocence. And even if you are to some extent culpable, I must admit my own failing in not immediately taking outrage at your confinement here. There is blame a-plenty to go around."

"Then I will say what I should have before. Flee this place before you to end up on my bench! Take your horse, go far and fast, and do not look back! It is too late for most of us, but you are able, strong of will, and have the advantage of your steed. You might yet escape!"

And indeed, there was nothing to anchor me to that terrible place, and every reason to leave. But I hesitated. "Not without you, at least. There are tools here, and I am stronger than any flesh-man. We will break your chain and be on our way!"

He shook his head. "I will not leave without poor Dead-weight, and even with the chain cut, he would slow your escape too much. No, you must go without me." And I could hear the sadness in his words. To deny his own freedom was breaking his heart, but he would not abandon his mechanical friend, and I knew then that I had chosen correctly in offering him mercy."

"Farewell, then," I said, slipping out the door, "and luck to you both." But as I did, with full intention to depart, I knew I could not completely abandon he or his companion, or any of the other poor retches who toiled at the Steam Man's house, or grounds, or in the dark depths of his mine. Yes, I would flee, but to tell the tale of this place, and to seek the aid of others in their eventual rescue and liberation.

My fear of discovery was greater now, and I turned down the flame in the lantern to the barest glow, just enough to pick my way through the coal piles without falling on my face. I headed back toward where I thought the path to the carriage house awaited, but soon found myself facing a impassible, black mountain of cold.

Somewhere I had taken a wrong turn. I retraced my steps, but soon again found myself in a blind canyon among the piles of black stone. I was about to retrace my steps when I heard the sound of a steam whistle, and the shouts of excited voices. There could be little doubt that my night-time adventure had been discovered!

I extinguished my lantern, and hearing the voices behind me, resolved that my best course was to climb the mountain of coal and try and place it between myself and pursuit. Barely able even to see the sky, I scrambled up the steep slope of loose coal by feel alone. A clockwork-man's sense of touch is seemingly poorer than a flesh-man's, and it works better on some materials than others. To my distress, I found that coal was one of those surfaces on which it worked poorly. I was able to find the sharp edges of the chunks, but the faces registered to my fingers and toes barely at all, and frequently I would find myself scrambling for purchase, sliding down the slope and sending cascades of chunk coal tumbling behind me. I was certain that at any moment the sound would give me away. But though I heard voices now and then, some far and some closer, I saw no lantern light indicating imminent capture.

Finally I reached the top of the pile, and stood cautiously on the ridge, eagerly locating the mine derrick that gave me some sense of location.

"There he is!" A voice shouted, and I recognized it as that of Copperpot.

In that terrible moment, I realized that in standing, I had doubtless presented my outline, stark against the star-lit sky. Before I could remedy that mistake, a bullet ricocheted off the top of my shoulder and whistled past the horn of my left ear. Thrown forward, I toppled into the darkness, smashing head-first into unseen coal, spinning head-over-heels, smashing my dented shoulder, then rolling helplessly, the largest participant in a growing avalanche.

After an eternity, the falling stopped and I lay half covered in coal. My escapement hammered in my chest, and the gears in my poor head screamed. Painfully, I pushed aside the coal, one lump at a time, until I saw something slightly less black that could only be sky, and also above me, an orange circle that I took to be a full Moon.

But the Moon had set before I reached the coal piles, and before my tortured gears could work it out, a firebox door swung open around the little circle, revealing it as the mica sight-hole over a firebox, and the Steam Man stood over me, dimly illuminated orange by his own reflected firelight.

———

The Steam Man seemed determined to make a show of my fate. Every worker in the winder-mill, upper mine, and house stood milling around me anxiously, lit by dozens of lanterns hung on the derrick itself and on nearby posts, and a summons had even been sent even to those workers deep in the mine. The supervisors were hauled up by a lift from the black pit under the derrick, but we were forced to wait as the rest of the miners apparently wound their way up through angled shafts I had not yet seen.

My hands were already tightly tied, and Copperpot threw a lasso of stout rope over my shoulders and cinched it tight just under my elbows, binding my arms tightly to my body.

The length of rope extending from the loop was taken by Kettle, who tossed it over a cross-beam in the derrick, grabbed the end as it swung back towards, him, and took up the slack. He gave it a little pull, and I found myself tugged half a step towards the waiting abyss.

I heard a disturbance in the assembled, and they parted like a curtain to make way for those shuffling out of the darkness. At last they came, those unfortunates who until then I had known only in my imagination: those poor wretches who in unimaginable black, with pick and shovel and worn fingers chipped at the mine face, filled the coal carts, sending them to the surface to meet their master's insatiable hunger.

They were all crusted black with coal dust, and they moved, slowly, painfully, as though the dust ground away at their joints with every movement. Despite their covering, I could see that they were all dented and scratched, and many had evidently suffered calamity in the mine. Most were patched together with mis-matched parts. Some were missing hands, or feet, or entire limbs. With them, lead by ropes, came mules, thin, sickly, such miserable creatures that to look upon them filled me with pain.

And as the vanguard of this decrepit hoard halted before me, I at last understood at last the bucket of eye-lenses I had seen in the workshop, for each of them had no more than one eye. Perhaps the Steam Man thought any more was unneeded in their light-deprived toil. And some had no eyes at all, lead stumbling along by their more fortunate companions.

I turned my gaze from this terrible sight to the Steam Man, on whom I had once looked upon with wonderment and delight, and whose visage now only wound my springs tight with rage. "What will you do with me now, monster? Am I to join these poor mechanical creatures in darkness and toil?"

The Steam Man laughed. "You would only plan your escape, or perhaps even attempt to rally my lowest servants against me. No, Artilleryman, that is not to be your fate. But whatever happens now is of your own making! I offered you friendship, and gave you opportunity to earn your trust. Instead, you have ably demonstrated your unworthiness of it!"

"Now that I have seen what terrors you are capable of, I would sooner melt in hell than call you friend!"

The Steam Man turned toward me. "So be it." He raised up one great foot, and like the connecting rod of a locomotive, it shot out and slammed into my chest, pitching me back into darkness. I am sure I let out a cry of alarm as I tumbled into the unmeasured depths, but my one thought in that moment was that I would not allow my tormentor the satisfaction of hearing me scream. Then I stopped with a great lurch that seemed nearly to snap me in half.

I had not reached bottom. Instead, I had been stopped by the rope around my middle, and I dangled, spinning in darkness, but for the dim square of sky far above. Then the rope lurched, and I expected to finally complete my plunge. But instead, I was drawn upwards a bit. And then again. And again and again. Finally I was pulled above the lip of the pit, and I could see Copperpot and Kettle at the other end of the rope, pulling me up hand-over hand until I hung with my feet well above the lip of the mine shaft.

"It's good you didn't drop me, Steam Man! If you mean to kill me anyway, then," I nodded toward the assembled miners, "there are many here who could use my parts."

The Steam Man laughed, a deep and terrible pipe-organ

laugh. "You are defiant, I will give you that, Artilleryman, and you continue to entertain. As such, it pains me to end your existence, so I offer you one last option. If you agree to serve me, I would keep you as my companion and jester of my court, but only so far as the trust you've learned will allow. As you say, you have parts others can use, and like this rough flesh-man I call mechanic, you need to be hobbled."

He rubbed his chin, as though considering. "I could have your legs removed, like Deadweight, so that you would serve as your own hobble!" He laughed again. "Perhaps two legs and an arm. A single arm should be enough for you to drag yourself around with! And besides, I might want to teach you to play chess!" His laughter roared and echoed through the black canyons of coal.

I admit, I was filled with dread. I had seen enough to know that his was no idle bluff. But if I was to meet my end, I was determined to give him no satisfaction. "Well then," I said, "you might just as well take my other arm too, and my mainspring, and my head too! For no part of me, no matter how diminished, would serve you, not while a single fork buzzes in my head, and while a single gear turns in my chest! Give my parts to these others, so that one day they can be inspired to rise up against you, to strike when lest suspect, draining your boiler dry, and choking your draft till your fires grow cold!"

The Steam Man stood silent, as we stood eye-to-eye. And in that moment, I think he saw that I would never yield. And in that moment, though it may be my imagination, it seemed that I saw fear in those featureless glass lenses.

He turned to Copperpot, and his hand started to raise in signal to loose me finally into the black pit.

But then their was a commotion behind the crowd, a whinny that echoed from a brass trumpet, and the thundering of metal hooves. Terrified, the assembled parted, and to my wondering eyes came the most welcome of sights from the darkness beyond.

"Piston!" I cried.

My great clockwork horse turned and charged straight toward me without hesitation or sign of fear, and in that moment, I conceived the most desperate and unworkable of plans. I kicked my knees apart and hoisted my boots up.

And somehow that miraculous war-horse seemed to sense my intent, as though the forks in our heads somehow vibrated the same tune, he redoubled his pace, charging directly at the edge of the pit.

With desperate haste, the Steam Man waved his signal and the rope began to slip through Copperpot and Kettle's slack fingers.

And at that moment, Piston lowered his head and lept out into space.

Though I have fled war, I am an Artilleryman still. I am quick of limb and understanding the movement of things flung through space comes as naturally to me as swimming to a fish. Time seemed to slow, as I saw in my head the gentle arc of Pison's flight almost directly under me. I twisted myself around, and reached out my right foot out just as his back slid between my parted legs.

The saddle on Piston's back is actually a curved metal plate bolted there, and I was able to hook first my right heel, then my left, under the bottom lip of it, pulling myself down to ride backwards.

I feared that my added weight might slow Piston too much

to gain purchase on the far side of the shaft, but he landed with his four hooves just on the edge, and scrambled on past the lip. We traveled another few feet, and then the rope snapped tight, yanking me so hard that I feared I might yet lose my legs that night.

Copperpot and Kettle had latched onto the moving rope and now held it tight to prevent my escape. But though we had slowed, Piston could not so soon halt his flight, and as the pulled threatened to snap me in half, Kettle was instead pulled over the edge into the pit. He screamed, and now hit full weight tore at me, trying to take me with him into death.

Unable to stop, Piston instead turned, spinning us and the rope around a post, sending the lantern hanging there crashing to the ground.

Pulled by Kettle's weight, unwilling or unable to release the line, Copperpot too was pulled into the pit, and his weight too was added to my burden.

Then, as I could take no more, Piston reared and snapped at the doubled-rope, snapping it with gun-metal teeth.

Copperpot and Kettle screamed for a long, long, time, until they were suddenly silenced by a crash far below.

I finally sat, backwards but secure on Piston's saddle. I leaned to my right as far as I could and extended out my wrists, just far enough so that Piston could turn back and chew through my bindings.

I considered my next move. I was outnumbered a hundred to one if the Steam Man's servants remained loyal to him, and I was still surrounded, unlikely to escape if that were the case. But they remained still, stunned and silent, uncertain what to make of this turn of events.

It was rather the Steam Man himself that concerned me.

He moved towards me around the outside of the mine shaft, clouds of smoke and steam puffing above him, gaining speed with each step like an accelerating locomotive. I had no gun, no weapon. I was more nimble, but I would never outrun him. He was twice my size, and in every other way my physical superior.

As he closed to within yards of us, there was but one choice.

"Piston! *Kick!*"

I saw those two great, metal, hooves lash out, striking like a pair of steam hammers, and I was nearly tossed from my perch, but that I had already squeezed my legs so hard around that saddle I felt I might have soldered myself there.

And the Steam Man staggered back, two steps, three, and teetered there a moment, arms waving madly. "Help me!" He cried.

But nobody did.

As he tumbled back into the blackness, I finally leapt from the saddle, landing on shaky legs and falling to my knees, looking down into the blackness as I saw the small, round, light of his firebox.

Then, brighter, as the firebox door flew open, coals and sparks spinning out like falling stars, strangely beautiful. I waited for the terrible crash.

It was not to come. All at once, the very air at the bottom of the shaft seemed to catch fire, and to my wondering eyes, I saw a rising cloud of fire form a wall and rush upwards to me. "Get back!" I cried, rolling clear and pulling myself to my feet, running as fast as I could, until a fist of air flattened me to the ground.

I rolled on my back, and looked up to behold a great

column of fire fading to black smoke, boiling into the sky, finally spreading out at the top of it, a giant breath of flame like the devil's last breath.

The wonderment of it held me for a moment, but then the burning derrick fell into the conflagration, and I saw the poles around the pit, though clear of the flames, were beginning to smolder. Mechanical men have little sense of cold or heat, and some of the braver onlookers were beginning to wander back, not appreciating the danger. I especially feared for the miners, who covered in coal dust, might themselves burst into flames.

I pulled myself properly onto Piston's saddle, and we rode in circles around the flaming pit, warning back those who came too close.

By the time the sun's red rays were peeking over the Kentucky hills, the fire had burned down a bit, but it had not gone out, and fueled as it was by the Earth itself, I feared it might not do so for years, if not decades. Black clouds still rolled up from the pit into the morning sky, turning the sun the color of blood.

I had been afeared that their master, dead, the throngs might turn on me, but as the sun rose, they fell quiet and still, seemingly uncertain what to do next. I sat astride Piston, reigns held loosely in my hands, equally uncertain. Then, with a clanking of chains, a familiar human face emerged from the crowd, Deadweight knuckle-walking behind him.

Joshua survey the scene, then punched his fist at the sky. "Liberty!" He yelled. "Liberty!"

Again and again he shouted the word, and others began to join in. "Liberty! Liberty!"

I did not know if they shouted my name, or proclaimed their freedom from servitude. Personally, I preferred the latter.

But in any case, it was a glorious noise, and it went on until the sun was well clear of the sky, until it broke like a wave on the shore, and they milled about, slapping each other on the back.

Joshua and Dreadweight came over, and I dismounted to speak with them.

Joshua smiled at me, and clasped my shoulders like an old friend. "You saved us, Liberty Brass! I did not think it possible, but you saved us!"

"What I have done, I have done by accident mostly," I said, "and with much aid from Piston here. And do not be grateful too soon, for if anything, I have delivered you from servitude into uncertainty."

"Then deliver us from that too, Liberty Brass! We need a leader here now. Stay with us!"

I shook my head and a laugh burst unbidden from my speaking-horn. "I'm barely fit to lead myself, much less anyone else! Besides, they can't stay here. None of them can."

He looked at me, puzzled.

I gestured at the rising smoke. "This plantation is sustained by coal, and while there is plenty on hand, there will be no reopening this mine. Eventually the coal will run out, and you cannot wind them all yourself."

He nodded sadly. "You are right, Liberty Brass. But I will do what I can to fix them up first. My part in this cannot be forgotten or forgiven. I must do what I can in reparation. I'll start by giving the miners back their lost eyes."

"And then they must leave, perhaps a few at a time, and seek new homes and new lives for themselves."

"Where can they go?"

I shook my head. "I have no idea. We are a new kind of

men, new to freedom. Perhaps here the miners are the most fortunate of us, as they are used to groping in darkness. As for myself, I head an unknown fate. I head only west, for I feel that is where new things must go."

Just then, I felt a tugging at my leg, and I knelt down to look Deadweight face to face.

To my surprise, he began to talk to me, his voice reedy, but gaining confidence as he spun his tale. "I have heard of a place," he said. "Only stories and rumors, but it is something. They say that years ago there was a steam man named Calliope Jones, not a cruel creature like the Steam Man, but a showman of great mirth and kindness. And one day, growing tired of his travels, he stumbled on the remains of an old grist mill in the Texas hills. It was on a river running clear and strong, and he built there first a winder-mill, and then a town, where outcasts of both metal and flesh were welcome and could all live as equals."

The story filled me with wonder. "Where is this place, Deadweight?"

"Perhaps only in dreams," he said, "but if it truly exists, I know only that it is in Texas."

"Then if it exists," I said, "I will find it. And if I find it, I will figure a way to get the word out, so that all of you could come."

Joshua nodded. "It might be just a dream, but it's a good one."

I stood and shook his hand. Then I looked down at Dread-weight. "Can you fix his legs?"

Joshua smiled wide, showing all his teeth. "At risk of my own head, I hid them away in a loft where the Steam Man couldn't find them, praying a day like this might come. He will stand tall again!"

I climbed back into the saddle. "You all will," I said. "Fare thee well!"

And Piston and I rode off into the rolling hills, until the black clouds of the Steam Man's tomb were lost behind us.

We rode west.

We rode towards hope.

NEWSLETTER SIGN-UP

DEAN WESLEY SMITH

Sign up for the Dean Wesley Smith newsletter, and keep up with the latest news, releases and so much more—even the occasional giveaway.

Go to **deanwesleysmith.com.**

Sign up for the WMG Publishing newsletter, too, and get the latest news and releases from all of the WMG authors and lines, including *Pulphouse Fiction Magazine, Smith's Monthly,* and so much more.

To sign up go to **wmgpublishing.com.**

Follow Dean on BookBub

ABOUT THE EDITOR

DEAN WESLEY SMITH

Considered one of the most prolific writers working in modern fiction, with more than 30 million books sold, *USA Today* bestselling writer Dean Wesley Smith published far more than a hundred novels in forty years, and hundreds of short stories across many genres.

At the moment he produces novels in several major series, including the time travel Thunder Mountain novels set in the Old West, the galaxy-spanning Seeders Universe series, the urban fantasy Ghost of a Chance series, a superhero series starring Poker Boy, and a mystery series featuring the retired detectives of the Cold Poker Gang.

His monthly magazine, *Smith's Monthly*, which consists of only his own fiction, premiered in October 2013 and offers readers more than 70,000 words per issue, including a new and original novel every month.

During his career, Dean also wrote a couple dozen *Star Trek* novels, the only two original *Men in Black* novels, Spider-Man and X-Men novels, plus novels set in gaming and television worlds. Writing with his wife Kristine Kathryn Rusch under the name Kathryn Wesley, he wrote the novel for the NBC miniseries The Tenth Kingdom and other books for *Hallmark Hall of Fame* movies.

He wrote novels under dozens of pen names in the worlds

of comic books and movies, including novelizations of almost a dozen films, from *The Final Fantasy* to *Steel* to *Rundown*.

Dean also worked as a fiction editor off and on, starting at Pulphouse Publishing, then at *VB Tech Journal*, then Pocket Books, and now at WMG Publishing, where he and Kristine Kathryn Rusch serve as series editors for the acclaimed *Fiction River* anthology series.

For more information about Dean's books and ongoing projects, please visit his website at www.deanwesley-smith.com and sign up for his newsletter.

For more information:
www.deanwesleysmith.com

f facebook.com/deanwsmith3
P patreon.com/deanwesleysmith
BB bookbub.com/authors/dean-wesley-smith

www.ingramcontent.com/pod-product-compliance
Lightning Source LLC
Chambersburg PA
CBHW010732100726
47899CB00009B/3009